A WORK OF ART

MELODY MAYSONET

Merit Press

Published by
Merit Press
an imprint of F+W Media, Inc.
10151 Carver Road, Suite 200
Blue Ash, OH 45242. U.S.A.
www.meritpressbooks.com

ISBN 10: 1-4405-8254-8
ISBN 13: 978-1-4405-8254-7
eISBN 10: 1-4405-8255-6
eISBN 13: 978-1-4405-8255-4

Printed in the United States of America.

10 9 8 7 6 5 4 3 2

Library of Congress Cataloging-in-Publication Data
Maysonet, Melody.
    A work of art / Melody Maysonet.
        pages cm
    ISBN 978-1-4405-8254-7 (hc) -- ISBN 1-4405-8254-8 (hc) -- ISBN 978-1-4405-
8255-4 (ebook) -- ISBN 1-4405-8255-6 (ebook)
    [1. Artists--Fiction. 2. Fathers and daughters--Fiction. 3. Sexual abuse--Fiction.] I. Title.
    PZ7.1.M39Wo 2015
    [Fic]--dc23
                                2014039495

This is a work of fiction. Names, characters, corporations, institutions, organizations, events, or locales in this novel are either the product of the author's imagination or, if real, used fictitiously. The resemblance of any character to actual persons (living or dead) is entirely coincidental.

Cover design by Sylvia McArdle.
Cover images © stillfx/123RF; Sergejs Rahunoks/123RF.

This book is available at quantity discounts for bulk purchases.
For information, please call 1-800-289-0963.

DEDICATION

For Dawn, my big sister and hero.

ACKNOWLEDGMENTS

Huge thank-yous to Joyce Sweeney and Jamie Morris, for teaching me about the craft of novel writing and for cheering me on in every stage. I'm also indebted to Joyce's Tuesday critique group, especially Joanne Butcher, Cathy Castelli, Faran Fagen, Stacie Ramey, Jonathan Rosen, and Mindy Weiss. Another critique group—Pam Morrell, Robert Ochart, Erica Orloff, and Jonathan Van Zile—saw this book in its earliest stages and helped me find my way.

To all the people of SCBWI: thank you for guiding me through the world of publishing. And to David R. and Victoria Trenton: thank you for guiding me through the labyrinths of the prison system.

I owe a debt of gratitude to my agent, Tina P. Schwartz, and my editor, Jacquelyn Mitchard, for taking a chance on a new writer and a tough subject. I hope I make them proud.

Lastly, I want to thank my family—including Mom, Dawn, Eva, Harrison, and Megan—for their unconditional love and support. I especially want to thank my husband, Adam, and my son, Caleb. You guys are the best family ever!

CHAPTER 1

Painting my dad was all about mood. Saturated blue for the sharp odor of paint. Muddy green for the faint whiff of mildew. Murky gray for the stink of ashes. A sparse room, textured like white noise, with crooked lines and lots of obtuse angles. Then in the center, the stretched shadow of a man. That was my dad.

Dad crushed out his cigarette and took the canvas from my hands. "This should be interesting." He held my painting at arm's length. "This is how you see me?"

"It's more of an abstract," I said.

"I don't like it." He turned the painting sideways and studied it some more. "It doesn't give off the right vibe."

I lifted the canvas out of his hands before he could launch into a full-blown critique. "What about that other one? The one where I'm, like, five years old, and you're watching me draw my own face."

"Yeah, much better. Is it down here?"

"In my room. I'll grab it when he gets here."

Dad looked around at the mess we'd made of his studio. The scattered piles of sketches, the canvases propped against walls. He liked things nice and neat. "I don't want your teacher coming down here," he said.

I swept some loose sketches into a pile and laid them on his desk. "I'll straighten up a little. I don't want Mr. Stewart hanging out upstairs. Mom's acting crazy."

He cocked an eyebrow at me.

"Okay, crazier than usual."

"Don't worry about your mom." He tapped the ends of his fingers together, each one ink-stained from his years as an illustrator. "She'll probably go hide as soon as he gets here."

I could only hope.

Dad pulled a sketch from one of the stacks on his desk. "What about this one?"

The paper was old and yellowing, the charcoal lines smeared. A man balanced a newborn baby on his lap like a cup of coffee that might spill. The baby lay naked and kicking. Tiny fists reached for the man's face. My dad's signature was scrawled in the corner.

"Is that you?" I asked. "And me?"

He grinned. "Not the typical father-daughter portrait."

"But I like it." I laid it on top of our growing pile. "They won't have room for all these."

"So we let them decide which ones to keep." He rooted out a sketchbook from the bottom of his stack. "This one's yours." He held it up so I could see the bent cover, stained with grease. A child's handwriting in black marker: *Tera Waters, age 9.*

Mine, yes. But how did he get it? I had a vague memory of throwing it away.

Dad rolled his office chair closer and folded back the cover.

"You didn't know, did you?"

"Know what?"

"How good you were."

His praise soaked into me like sunlight. I moved closer, stepping behind his chair so I could look over his shoulder.

He turned the pages, the paper so thick it fanned the air. When I was little, I sketched everything in my world. The giant stuffed lion Dad got from the Goodwill when he was too broke to buy Christmas presents. My friend Haley from across the street, before she ditched me for new friends. My black lab that ran away.

Dad paused when he got to a drawing of Mom digging in her garden. She looked like she was trying to kill the earth with her trowel. He turned another page, and there was my nine-year-old face crowding the paper with its gaping eyes and narrow jaw. An ugly kid, but I didn't know it yet, so I drew myself true to life.

"Amazing," Dad murmured.

They *were* pretty good, especially for a nine-year-old. But I didn't like them. They felt wrong, like the slick of grease staining the cover.

Overhead, Mom's footsteps thumped across the kitchen floor. Cupboard doors slammed.

Dad rolled his eyes to the ceiling. "Crazier than usual?"

"Definitely."

"Does she know your teacher's coming?

"I told her yesterday, but who knows if she remembers."

"She does, but she'll pretend she doesn't." He fingered the unturned pages of the sketchbook. "Am I in here anywhere?"

"I doubt it. Can we please look at something else?"

"In a minute."

He turned another page, and suddenly I couldn't breathe. The drawing in his hands sucked the air out of my throat.

I stared at the pencil sketch of my room, the details so familiar. The flowered wallpaper, the plastic reading trophies, the Powerpuff Girls bedspread.

And on the bed, a girl. Naked.

A naked girl crouched on all fours. Her whole body laid bare, her face pointed at the wall.

She could have been anyone or no one. But *I* knew who she was. My dad knew, too. The naked girl was me.

I stared at her. She should be long gone. Incinerated. Ashes. The drawing and the photo that went with it. I opened my mouth to say it, but then the door at the top of the stairs creaked open and Mom yelled down, "Tera!"

Now what? She sounded close to panic.

"What are you *doing?*" she screeched. "You should be gone already!"

Not now, Mom. I ripped the page from the sketchbook, felt the rip all the way to my bones.

Dad watched me, his eyebrows raised. "So not one of your favorites?"

"Tera!" Mom's voice jarred me. "I need those groceries!"

The sketch in my grip felt noxious. I wanted to rip it into tiny pieces, burn it, bury the ashes.

But Mom was calling me, and I knew better than to ignore her. "I can't leave!" I called back. "Mr. Stewart is on his way over."

"What are you talking about?" she yelled.

"He'll be here any second. I'll go after."

"After *what*?"

Dad reached for his cigarettes. "You better talk to her. Get to her before she implodes."

He was right. If I didn't try to calm her, she'd ramp up to maximum shrillness, and that was the last thing I wanted Mr. Stewart to see. Well, almost the last thing. My hand stiffened around the sketch. I couldn't look at it again.

"Tera!"

"I'm coming!" I crushed the sketch into a tight ball and stuffed it in the wastebasket under my dad's desk. I thought he might look at me, say something, but he went back to sorting sketches like nothing had happened. Was I overreacting? Didn't all artists draw themselves in the nude?

No time to ponder. Mom was waiting. I kept my footsteps light, my face cheery. I didn't want her going off in front of Mr. Stewart.

She whirled on me as soon as I set foot in the kitchen. "Who's Mr. Stewart?"

Half the cupboards hung open. The kettle on the stove leaked steam. An overflowing mug sat next to the stove, a teabag staining the counter. I smelled clove. One of her calming teas, but it obviously wasn't doing its job. She was as frantic as ever, but at least she'd brushed her hair and changed out of the t-shirt she'd been wearing for the past two days.

"My art teacher." I struggled to keep my voice calm as I grabbed a dishcloth and scrubbed at the tea stain. "He's picking up those paintings for that article in *ArtWorld*."

"He's coming now?"

"Yeah, Mom, he's—"

"Why can't you send photos? You have photos of all that stuff."

"Because they want originals." I made myself stop scrubbing. "You won't even know he's here. You can go lie down until he leaves."

"I don't want to lie down. I want you to call him and tell him not to come. Call him from the car." She scooped up her car keys and shoved them at me.

I didn't take them. "He's on his way already. He'll be here any minute."

"Why, Tera?" The keys rattled in her hand. "Why today?"

"They need pictures for the article."

"You said they interviewed you already. You told me that last week."

I clenched my jaw, trying hard to keep from snapping at her. "They want to show our *art*, Mom. The article's about father-and-daughter *artists*."

The door leading down to Dad's studio swung open. Dad sidled up to us and leaned against the counter. "What's going on?"

"Mom doesn't want Mr. Stewart coming over."

"Her art teacher won't hurt you, Connie. If he scares you that much, you can go hide."

I flashed him a look. Why did he always have to set her off? "He won't stay long," I told her. "I promise."

I don't think she heard me. I don't even think she was aware of me. She was staring out the picture window that faced the street. A car was turning into our driveway.

"That's him." I touched her arm, hoping it would reassure her. "It'll be okay."

Mom bit her lip. I couldn't look at her as I crossed the living room toward the door. *Please, Mom. Please, be good.*

A car door slammed. Footsteps on gravel. Shoes thumping on the wooden porch. This was it. I pasted on a smile and opened the door before Mr. Stewart could knock.

For a second, I didn't know what to say. He'd been my art teacher and mentor since the beginning of high school, so in my mind he walked on a higher plane of existence. Greeting him on my doorstep brought him down to earth.

"*Bonjour!*" I finally said, my voice too loud. I always talked loudly when I was nervous. "*Comment ça va?*"

"Practicing your French?" The thick-rimmed glasses Mr. Stewart wore made his eyes look twice their size. It was hard to believe I'd had a crush on him my freshman year.

"I'm trying," I said. "But my accent's horrible. Any idea what I said?"

"Not a clue." He smiled to let me know he was kidding. "You'll do fine. Just think about painting the same gardens as Monet. Think about how wonderful it's going to feel to be immersed in that culture of art."

Like I could ever forget. It didn't seem real yet, the fact that I'd be studying in *Paris*! Whatever crappy thing was going on in my life didn't matter, because being at the art institute would make everything okay. Only a few more months and I'd be there—away from here—surrounded by people who understood me, making actual friends because everyone there would have the same interests as me.

Mr. Stewart gestured outside, to the mass of trees and bushes choking our yard. "This is worth painting, too. Who's the gardener?"

I followed his gaze, trying to see beauty in the tangled mess of green. "My mom. But not anymore. It's way overgrown."

"*C'est très belle.*"

"I guess, maybe."

"Your parents are home?"

"They're in here." I led Mr. Stewart to the kitchen, my stomach wired for the worst. Dad was nowhere in sight, and Mom had her back to us, staring out the window that faced the driveway.

"Mom?" I kept my voice gentle.

When she didn't turn around, Mr. Stewart cleared his throat. "It's been such a pleasure," he said, "teaching your daughter."

She kept quiet, still looking out the window. At least the silence was better than shrieking.

Mr. Stewart's smile slipped, but it came back when Dad appeared from the hallway. Dad stepped in front of Mom and held out his hand to Mr. Stewart. "I'm Tera's dad. Tim Waters."

"So nice to meet you." Mr. Stewart looked relieved as he shook Dad's hand. "I'm a big fan. I love the *After End* series."

"I'm surprised you've heard of it," Dad said.

"Tera told me how popular it was, so I did some investigating." Mr. Stewart shoved his hands into the pockets of his blazer. "I haven't read graphic novels since my college days, but your work seems very fresh."

I could tell Dad liked the praise, even though he acted like he didn't. "Well, I'm a long way from being famous," he said.

I chimed in: "But he signs autographs all the time."

Mom made a choking sound from the window. We all ignored her.

"At comic-book conventions," Dad added. "Not in the real world."

"Well, you know the saying," said Mr. Stewart. "Those that can, do. Those that can't, teach."

"Or starve," Dad said. "I did plenty of time as a starving artist."

Mr. Stewart shook his head like he didn't quite believe that. "And now you're sending your daughter to Paris. To what is arguably the best art institute in the world."

"It *is* the best. I read it on their website."

They both laughed. At least *something* was going well. Dad and Mr. Stewart chatted, and Mom paced in front of the window like a prisoner in a jail cell. Mr. Stewart was polite enough to pretend he didn't notice.

"Dad," I said. "Why don't you take Mr. Stewart to the living room while I get those paintings." I gave him a look and flicked my eyes toward Mom.

Dad took the hint. He led Mr. Stewart to the couch. I could still see them from the kitchen, but at least they weren't in the same room with Mom.

I squeezed her arm. "I'll hurry."

Her eyes were locked on the window. "It's too late."

Too late? I finally followed her gaze to see what in the world was so fascinating.

And that's when the first police car turned down the driveway.

CHAPTER 2

Another police car pulled in behind the first, then a third.

Three cop cars for one house. For *my* house.

"Mom?" I tried to sound casual, but my voice was too high. "Why are the cops here?"

And just like that, conversation in the living room stopped. Dad poked his head over the counter that divided the two rooms, a meerkat sensing danger. "What's going on?" he asked.

Mom must have known they were coming, but she didn't answer. Whatever it was, it couldn't be good. Not with three police cars.

Voices from the porch, then a pounding on the door. Dad's head disappeared behind the counter. Mom didn't move.

"You want me to answer it?" I heard my voice, and it sounded so calm. Maybe because Mr. Stewart was sitting on the couch, watching the whole thing. If I acted like nothing was wrong, nothing would *be* wrong.

I crossed the room in silence. Everything felt hazy, like walking in a dream. The hand opening the door seemed like someone else's hand.

And then the door swung wide, and the world became sharp and real. A black man and a pretty white woman stood frowning at me from the doorway. The woman held up the badge that hung around her neck. "I'm Agent Caine. This is Officer Jenks." She gazed past me, into the living room. "Are your parents home?"

"Um." I turned back to the living room, saw a blur of staring faces. "They're right here."

Dad rose from the couch. Smiling. But I saw how his neck tightened, his arms hanging like dead limbs. "Can we take this outside?" His voice polite. Friendly. Nothing in the world to worry about.

"No, we can't," Caine said. "You're Timothy Waters?"

Dad's eyes swept the room, like maybe one of us might swap identities with him. Mom had backed herself into a corner, her knuckles pressed to her lips. Mr. Stewart sat rigid on the couch, fingers digging into his knees. I still gripped the doorknob, my feet glued to the carpet.

"Yes, I'm Tim Waters." He cleared his throat. "What's this about?"

Caine pulled a document from her jacket pocket and handed it to my dad like she was dealing him a card. "It's a warrant," she told him. "We're searching the house."

Dad stared at the warrant, his face pale. Caine and Jenks stepped aside as three more uniformed cops brushed past me. They talked to each other in low voices as they pulled on latex gloves.

I gripped the door, solid beneath my hands. Real. This was real.

A warrant meant they were looking for something. But what? Drugs? The only drugs I'd ever seen were the legal kind, the ones for Mom's depression and anxiety. Did Dad steal something? I couldn't imagine what, since he hardly left the house. And it wasn't like we were rich.

"Mom, what's going on? What are they looking for?"

She swallowed, turned her head the other way.

"Dad, what does the warrant say?"

His shoulders tensed, but he didn't answer.

I let go of the door, took a stumbling step toward the closest cop. My eyes found his badge. *Jenks.*

"Please." I heard the fear in my own voice. "What are you searching for?"

He didn't look at me either.

Caine pointed at two of the cops. "Go search the bedrooms," she told them. When they disappeared down the hallway, she turned to Dad. "Where's your office, Mr. Waters?"

Dad said nothing.

Caine's eyelids fluttered, annoyed. Her eyes darted past Mr. Stewart on the couch, landed on my mom, still in the corner. "Ma'am?"

Mom seemed ready to talk, her first words since they arrived. "His studio is downstairs," she said. "In the basement."

And suddenly I knew what was happening. Mom had called the cops to get Dad in trouble. That was why she wouldn't look at me. She had probably planted something in his studio.

I cleared my throat. "Wait! If my mom called you here, it was a mistake. Tell them, Dad."

Dad shot me a look. Gratitude? Hope? "She's right. My wife's off her meds. She doesn't think straight when she's off her meds."

Caine gave a faint smile. She didn't believe us.

"Mom, tell them it's a mistake." If she told them now, this could all go away. But her lips stayed pressed together. She wasn't talking anymore.

When Mr. Stewart cleared his throat from the couch, it suddenly hit me that he was *here*, seeing this. Shame fell over me like a black sheet.

"Tera," he said. "You should sit down. Wait for it to be over."

I pretended not to hear. I didn't want to sit and wait. I had to do something.

I lurched toward my dad, but Jenks blocked my way with his arm. Stop.

"Why?" I pleaded. "Why can't I go to him?"

Then one of the cops searching the bedrooms came tromping back with my green laptop under his arm.

"What'd you find?" Caine asked.

"Just a laptop. I think it's the girl's."

It *was* mine. I reached out, knowing it was useless. "What are you doing with it?"

No one answered me. The cop with my laptop started opening kitchen drawers. Another cop searched the antique desk in the hallway where my parents kept important papers. I heard voices from Dad's studio, things being moved around. Then silence. The silence went on for a long time. Jenks gave a questioning look to Caine. She shrugged.

The two cops searching my dad's studio came stomping back up the stairs. One of them carried the hard drive from Dad's computer. The other had a sheaf of sketches thrown into a cracked leather binder. Dad hated when his drawings got creased, but his head was down, so he didn't see. He didn't see the crumpled drawing on top.

The sketch I had wadded into a ball not ten minutes ago. The sketch of the naked girl. They thought Dad drew it. They thought he was some kind of perv.

Jenks stepped around me. The next thing I knew, Dad's arms were being wrenched behind his back. I saw his face as the handcuffs snapped around his wrists. Eyes squeezed shut, lips pinched tight.

"Timothy Waters," said Jenks. "You are under arrest for possession of child pornography."

What?

My vision zoomed out, and for a split second, I saw my dad the way a stranger might—a creepy, sullen-faced thug who deserved what he got. But this was my *dad*, and he didn't deserve this. *I* was the one who drew the naked girl, not him.

I reached out a hand. "Wait a minute!" But when Caine looked at me, my throat closed up. The old secret clawed at my gut. If I said something, they'd know. I threw the photo out years ago because I didn't want anyone to see it. But maybe the digital file still haunted Dad's hard drive. Was that why they took his computer?

I finally found my voice. "You can't do this!"

Jenks gripped Dad by his elbows and led him toward the door. Dad stumbled like a sleepwalker.

"Mom, tell them!"

Still, she wouldn't look at me. No one looked at me.

"Please!" I cried. "He didn't do anything!"

They were out the door. I stumbled after them, squinting in the bright sunlight. Dad's feet got tangled on the porch steps. I couldn't help him, but I reached out anyway.

And that's when I saw Haley across the street. Watching.

Our eyes met as she tossed a lock of dark, waist-long hair over her shoulder. I felt myself shrink into a tiny speck. If the wind blew, it could carry me away.

Dad craned his neck to look at me. Scared. Not the Dad I knew. "Go back inside," he told me.

I didn't go back inside, though, even when he kept stumbling and the cops had to help him down the driveway. I watched his humiliation. Because turning my head felt too much like abandoning him.

CHAPTER 3

Self-Portrait

Sunlight brightened the kitchen table where Tera sat waiting with her paper and crayons. Her dad put his leather bag on the floor and sat beside her. He smelled like paint. Better than her mom's flowers.

She opened her drawing pad and held it to her nose. Paper was another good smell.

Her dad was shaking his head. "That cheapo paper is for kindergarteners."

"But I'm in kindergarten." Maybe he forgot how big she was.

"Not today you're not. Today you're an artist."

He reached into his leather bag, the one he carried with him everywhere, and slid out a thick pad of paper. This was the special paper, the stuff she wasn't allowed to borrow when she wanted to draw horses. She leaned in closer as he opened the pad. He flipped through drawings of all kinds of things—trees with kites stuck in them, men with swords, monsters with sharp teeth. All of them so good. She'd never be that good.

He stopped flipping pages when the drawings ran out and all that was left was blank paper. His hand slapped down on a page of clean white. "What do you see?"

At first she didn't see anything, but she leaned closer, just to make sure. That's when she noticed how the paper wasn't really white. Up close she saw gray and red and blue threads, all tight and mashed together.

"It looks dirty," she said.

"*Not dirty, but not pure either. That's your blank slate. Tabula rasa.*" *He smoothed his big hand over the paper. Took her hand and did the same. "Feel that?"*

"*It's bumpy.*"

"*Right. That's real life. This is what you draw on. Those little bumps give your drawing texture.*"

She didn't know what texture was, but that didn't matter. He was sitting here next to her, teaching her stuff. She pulled her box of crayons closer.

"*No crayons. Not today. Use this.*" *He handed her a pencil. Not a fat pencil with an eraser, but a thin one with a flat top and a point that looked sharp enough to cut.*

"*What if I mess up?*"

"*No big deal. Artists learn from their mistakes.*"

"*They do?*"

"*And disguise them sometimes. Do you know what that means?*"

"*They hide them.*"

"*Right. Or turn them into something else.*"

"*So no eraser?*"

"*Erasers are for babies.*"

Could that be true? She saw lots of grownups with erasers.

He tore a sheet from the pad. "Today I'll use the tear-out sheet. You draw in the sketchpad."

He slid the pad of special paper over so it was right there in front of her. That made her feel proud, like maybe it was hers, not his.

"*Now, when you're drawing a face, you want to get the proportions right—unless you're Pablo Picasso.*" *He smiled, and she smiled, too. Because her dad made a joke and Pablo Picasso was someone important.*

She watched him draw an oval on the paper, watched him cut the oval into four pieces with a cross.

"*This is where you put the eyes.*" *He pointed to the top pieces of the cross. "This is where the nose goes, and this is for the mouth.*"

She drew an oval on the sketchpad, making sure to get it right. Then she drew a cross on it.

Already he was filling in his oval with eyes, the beginning lines for a nose, a slit where the mouth would be.

"I started learning by drawing myself," he told her. "That's a good way for you to learn, too."

"You want me to draw me?"

"I love to draw you."

His hand moved over the page, making little strokes with the pencil, using his thick fingers to smudge black lines into gray. In only a few minutes, the oval with the cross turned into a face—her face. The way it looked when she saw herself in the mirror.

"That's a portrait," he said. "And when you draw yourself, it's called a self-portrait."

"It's good," she said, because that's what you said when you liked what another kid was coloring. She wanted to say something else, something that would let him know how good it really was, but she didn't have the right words.

"Now you try it." He guided her hand to the first cross section of her oval. "Right there. Draw your eyes."

She squeezed the thin pencil, pressed the sharp tip down on the paper—too hard. The point broke off.

"Careful. Don't try so hard. Let it flow the way you think it should feel."

She tried again. Already she could tell hers wouldn't be as good as his, but maybe he'd still be proud of her. She drew a circle for an eye and added eyelashes, then another circle for the other eye. The nose came next—easy except for the nostrils, which turned out way too big. The mouth came last. She drew a smiley face, then round circles. The circles she colored gray, for rosy cheeks.

"Is that you?" he asked.

"Do you like it?"

"Hmm." He leaned back and tilted his head. "You'll get better."

His hand flashed across the paper. A sharp rip and the page came out. Like pulling a loose tooth. Quick hurt and then it was over.

The thick pad of special paper went back in his bag. So did his pencil, but not the one he had let her borrow. That one she kept under the table. Maybe he'd forget to take it back.

He did *forget. He forgot her drawing, too. But that didn't matter so much. Her heart felt excited when she looked at what she'd done. A self-portrait.*

She pulled it closer. Maybe later she'd get an eraser and fix it. Maybe later her dad would hang it on the fridge.

CHAPTER 4

I stood on the porch, numb. The police cars were gone. Haley was gone too.

And Dad. What was happening to him? They were taking him to jail, and I had no idea what to do. Would they let him go once he explained? Would Mom and I have to bail him out? Did Mom and Dad even have enough money for something like that? And who were we supposed to call to make things happen?

I shivered in the cool breeze. A squirrel dashed up the porch steps. It stopped, its tail rippling, and then it was off, leaping for the nearest tree. Somewhere in the neighborhood, a child shrieked with laughter. And somewhere in a police car, Dad sat in handcuffs, on his way to jail.

I squeezed my eyes shut. I should have told them it was me in the drawing. Me in the photo.

If the photo even existed. I thought it was long gone.

I should have explained how it happened, and now it was too late.

Someone came up beside me on the porch. I opened my eyes. Mr. Stewart. He looked up at the darkening sky with his arms folded. Finally, he spoke.

"Do you need anything, Tera?"

I did, but already he'd seen too much. I was so embarrassed that I couldn't look at him. If I didn't speak, maybe he'd go away.

He waited another few seconds. "All right then." He started down the porch steps, stopped and looked back. "I'm sorry this happened to you."

I pressed my lips together and nodded, afraid of what noise I might make if I opened my mouth.

● ● ●

Mom sat at the table with two bottles of pills and a glass of water. Back in the day, she was pretty, but now she looked old and worn-out. I knew she couldn't help the way she was, but sometimes I got sick of tiptoeing around her moods.

And today wasn't a day to call her out. I needed her to stay calm. She had to take back whatever she told the police. They had to know—whatever she thought Dad did—it wasn't a big deal.

I sat across from her at the table, tried to smile. "You look like you're feeling better," I said. Which was true, even though her hands shook as she lifted her glass.

"I have a new doctor," she said. "We're trying something different." Mom was always trying something new for her depression and her "panic attacks," as she called them. New pills, mostly. Most of them didn't work. Either that or she quit taking them.

"That's good." I took a breath. The air inside the house felt sweaty. "Mom, you need—"

"Stop." Her glass thumped to the table.

"What am I doing?"

"You're not listening, that's what. I tried to get you to leave before they got here, but you never listen to me."

Suddenly I wanted to grab her glass of water and throw it in her face. I was sick of her mental excuses. *She* was to blame for this. They arrested Dad because *she* called them. And if this whole thing was about that photo—if it even existed—then she was mostly to blame for that, too. Because of her, I had to practice drawing nudes in secret.

"You don't make any sense," I said. "That's why I don't listen to you."

"So you're taking his side."

"Someone has to."

Outside, the wind picked up. Another spring storm. I stood.

"Where are you going?"

"To get my laptop."

"Your laptop's gone."

And then I remembered. The police took it. I sank into my chair. Now what? My antique phone didn't have Internet, and I had no idea how to get Dad out on bail.

"Did they leave a number for the jail?" I asked.

"You can't bail him out, if that's what you're thinking. You're too young, for one thing. And they're not going to let him go."

"You don't know that!"

"You'd be surprised what I know."

"So you won't even try?"

She took a sip of water. So smug, now that she thought she'd won. "He can rot in there for all I care."

Thunder rumbled in the distance. I clenched my hands into fists, tried to think. Maybe I could get someone else to bail him out.

Her fingers tapped her glass. "You think I wanted this to happen, don't you?"

I stared out the window. The sky was thick with gray clouds. Tornado weather. "I think you're jealous," I said.

"What are you talking about?"

"Dad and I get this big article written about us, and you can't stand it. You want to punish him. You hate to see me happy."

"You know that's not true."

"Then why, Mom? Tell me why you go against everything Dad does."

"It's not like that." She bowed her head, her fingers squeezing the glass. "I found something on his computer."

So she *did* find it. The photo of me naked. A gust of wind sent a branch scraping against the window, like nails on a chalkboard.

"Mom, I know what you're thinking."

Her voice turned vicious, and she jabbed a finger at me. "Don't tell me you know anything about this! Don't tell me that!"

I blinked, startled by the sudden force of her anger. "I won't. I wasn't going to."

"Because I can't deal with that right now."

"Fine." I clenched my jaw to keep from yelling at her. For every second we sat here fighting, Dad's nightmare got more real. Would they strip-search him? Take away his belt and shoelaces? I forced myself to breathe, to think.

Would they let him go if I told them it was my fault, that I did it to practice drawing the human form?

Her voice cut into my thoughts. "You can't help him, Tera."

"That's not true. I'll go visit him. Find out what to do."

"They won't let you see him without a parent. You're not even eighteen."

"You can take me."

She picked up one of her pill bottles and pretended to read the label.

"Mom, you have to take me. I need to talk to him. He needs to know."

"Know what?" A growl of thunder vibrated the table. "That you follow him around like a puppy dog? That you'll do anything he wants you to do?"

"That's not true! You're just making shit up!"

She slammed the pill bottle on the table. "Then tell me! Tell me what you think he needs to know."

That I don't blame him. That I'm out here trying to help him.

But I didn't say that. I didn't say anything while the first raindrops of the storm splattered the window. It's not like she would have listened.

CHAPTER 5

I took the phone book to my room and closed the door. The number for the county jail was listed in the "important numbers" section. I copied it into my notebook and checked my watch. Dad had been gone for almost an hour.

It took a few minutes to get through the jail's automated voice system, but finally I got a live person. She sounded old. "Central Intake," she said. "How can I help you?"

"Um." Where to start? "My dad got arrested, and I was wondering what I need to do to bail him out."

The woman on the phone must have felt sorry for me.

"When was he arrested?" she asked.

"About an hour ago."

"So that means he hasn't been processed yet."

"How long does that take?" I asked.

"Well, it varies. An officer will put his information into a computer. He'll see a nurse. He'll be fingerprinted."

"So this could take hours."

"It usually does. And he'll have his photo taken, too."

"You mean like a mug shot?"

"That's right. So after the whole booking process, he'll have his arraignment hearing. But that won't happen till tomorrow."

"I'm sorry." I had to be trying her patience. "What's an arraignment hearing?"

"That's when he stands before the judge and the judge decides on a bond."

"A bond?"

"The amount it'll take to bail him out."

"Oh."

"Some crimes have a standard bond attached to them. What'd they bring him in for, hon? I might be able to tell you the amount before he sees the judge."

"Do I have to say it?" There was no way I could say it.

"You don't have to say anything. Just wait till he's arraigned tomorrow and call back. They'll tell you how much the bond is."

"Okay. And what's, like, a standard bond amount?"

"It depends on what they brought him in for. It could be ten thousand. It could be a lot more than that."

"Ten thousand *dollars?*"

"I know. It sounds like a lot. But if you can't come up with the cash bond, call a bail bondsman. They put the money up, and you pay them a percentage. If your dad doesn't appear at his summons, the bail bondsman is liable for the bail amount, so sometimes they ask for collateral."

"So I don't have to come up with the bail money myself?"

"Not if you use a bail bondsman. You pay the bondsman a percentage. It's usually fifteen percent of the bond amount."

I did some quick math. I'd be looking at fifteen hundred dollars if Dad's bond was ten thousand. I couldn't imagine it being more than that.

"Can I visit him before he sees the judge tomorrow?" I asked. "Are there, like, visiting hours?"

"How old are you, honey?"

"Seventeen. I'll be eighteen in two weeks."

"You're a minor. You'd have to be accompanied by a parent or legal guardian."

So Mom was right.

"Call tomorrow," she said. "Find out what his bond is and then have your mom or someone who's of legal age call a bail bondsman."

"I can't call myself?"

"You're not an adult, honey. So you have two choices. Choice number one is to pay the cash bond yourself. If you do that, the courts will pay you back after your dad shows up for his summons. Or choice number two: Get an adult to contract with a bail bondsman."

"Okay."

"Any other questions?"

"I don't think so. Thank you for your help."

"That's all right, honey. Good luck."

After she hung up, I looked down at my notebook where I'd written only one thing: *Night in jail.*

I tore out the sheet and crumpled it into a ball. My room had gotten dark. Was Dad's jail cell dark, too? Were people being rough with him? Was he as scared as me?

I looked at the clock. On a normal night, I'd be finishing my homework. Instead, I kept reliving the nightmare: how the police had held my dad's elbows and shoved him out the door. Dad bent forward with his head down, me following behind, my mouth flapping as I pleaded with the cops. Dad casting a look back at me, stumbling a little. Me holding my stomach and hoping I'd wake up.

And in the back of my mind was another worry, slowly eating its way forward.

Haley saw. How long would it be before she blabbed to the whole school?

This had to end. I had to bail him out. And it wasn't like Mom would hand over her ATM card—not that my parents had any money to spare.

But I had money, thanks to Dad. The twenty thousand dollars he gave me so I could go to a good art school. I could use some of it to pay the bail bondsman. And then I could start working again at my old job. I'd have almost six months to replenish my bank account before I went to Paris.

But first I had to find out how much the bond was. And then I had to find someone who'd be willing to go to a bail bondsman for me. I turned eighteen in less than two weeks, but Dad couldn't wait that long.

Obviously, Mom wasn't going to help, and Dad didn't have any family besides us. He didn't have any friends, either, at least none that I knew about. He worked freelance, so it wasn't like he saw people at the office every day. And if I called one of his editors, they might end his contract over something like this. So who did that leave?

As much as I dreaded asking him, Mr. Stewart seemed like the only choice. I'd spent the last four years of high school trying to impress him, and the last year bragging to him about my dad's success. So asking him to bail out my dad from jail would have to rank in my top two most humiliating experiences—right behind him seeing my dad get arrested.

I told myself that now wasn't the time to be proud.

• • •

When I left for school the next morning, the air outside was thick with the odor of mud and earthworms. I waited at the top of my driveway for the bus, staying out from under the trees so the leaves wouldn't drip on the painting I carried. Mr. Stewart left yesterday without taking any of my artwork for the magazine. Bringing him one of my paintings gave me the perfect excuse to talk to him about my dad.

I peeked under the drop cloth I'd thrown over my painting and let myself imagine, just for a second, how it would look on the pages of *Art World*. I had painted it a few months ago, an impressionist-style piece called *Gray Day*. It showed a girl at a playground on a rainy day, her coat unbuttoned, her hair wet and straggly. All around her, kids in rain boots and raincoats laughed and chased each other, but she stood in the shadow of a towering metal slide, gazing at her own warped reflection in the mud puddle at her feet.

I covered the canvas again when I heard Haley and her mom leaving their house. I looked across the street. Mrs. Sweeney was digging in her purse, but Haley waved to me and smiled. Like we were still best friends. Like she hadn't told me back in fifth grade to get away from her and stop following her around.

Haley left her mom to wait by their Audi and hurried over to me, her long hair billowing. I looked up the street, hoping to see the bus rounding the corner. No such luck. I braced myself.

"Are you okay?" she asked, her eyes wide with fake concern. "I saw the police here yesterday."

"I'm fine."

"Well, what happened? With your dad?"

I knew she'd ask. I knew what to say. "It was a mistake." I shrugged. "He's coming home this afternoon."

"A mistake? You mean, they arrested the wrong person?"

"I don't know." Still no bus in sight. "I'll find out more today."

"But what'd they arrest him for?"

The sun rose above the rooftops. I had to squint to see her. "Drugs," I said.

"Your dad's a druggie?"

"I didn't say that. I said it was a mistake."

She pursed her lips together. A prissy smile. "I guess it could have been worse."

What did she mean by that? Did she know what they were accusing him of?

"Haley!" Mrs. Sweeney called. "Time to go!"

"Just a minute! I'm talking!"

I smiled at Mrs. Sweeney. To let her know how everything was fine and normal at the Waters household. She didn't smile back.

Haley smoothed her hair from her forehead. "If you ever want to talk . . ."

"Yeah," I said. "I know where you live."

"Seriously, Tera."

"Yeah, okay." As if I'd really open up to her, after the way she ended our friendship.

"Haley, come on!" Her mom again. "You're making me late!"

Haley rolled her eyes. "I have to go. Good luck with your dad."

I hugged my painting to my chest and watched her jog across the street to her mom. Mrs. Sweeney looked pissed. She said something I couldn't hear.

But Haley's voice was loud. "I'm not bothering her," she said. "I'm allowed to talk to her. And you're always nagging me for . . ." The roar of the bus engine drowned out the rest of her words. Her hands sliced the air as she talked.

Haley was still complaining when her mom passed her the car keys. Didn't she know how good she had it?

• • •

I loved the art room. I loved the smell of paint and turpentine and paper. I felt at home there, where every surface of every wall was covered in student art.

Mr. Stewart didn't have a class until second period, so I knew he'd be alone that morning. He stopped rummaging in his supply cabinet when he heard me come in.

"Hey, Tera." He studied my face. Cautious. "What's on your mind?"

"You left yesterday without taking anything for the magazine." I held up my painting. "So I brought you *Gray Day*. It was all I could carry on the bus."

"Oh." He took a long time closing the supply cabinet door. "About that."

"You don't like it?"

"You know I do. It's one of my favorites. It's just . . ." He took the painting and propped it against the wall. "I don't know if the article will see print."

I'd been looking forward to that article for months. When they interviewed me, I felt like a real artist, someone with a future. Disappointment stabbed me in the gut. "Why not?" I asked.

"Well, because . . ." He frowned.

"Because of what happened with my dad? The whole thing was a mistake."

"That may be, but it's about perceptions. I doubt the editor would take the risk."

"But that's not fair!"

"It might be that she'll postpone the article, just until this thing with your dad gets cleared up."

"But did you talk to her? The editor? How would she even know?"

He scratched his neck. "I thought it best she know all the facts about what she's getting into."

I tasted anger. Like biting down on foil. "The facts? There are no facts. My dad didn't do anything."

"I just . . . The editor's my friend, Tera. I can't let her publish something that might hurt her magazine."

"But that's stupid! It's not going to hurt her magazine!"

"Well, you're probably right, but it's her decision. If, like you say, it gets cleared up, we can call her. *I'll* call her. Tell her it was a mistake. Then I'm sure she'll go ahead with the article."

I lowered my head and clenched my teeth, trying to bite back anger. I couldn't be angry. I still needed his help.

"Does that sound fair, Tera?"

I nodded, swallowed, lifted my chin. "I need to talk to you about something."

"Okay." Again that caution.

"You asked me yesterday if I needed anything."

He nodded.

"And I need you to go to a bail bondsman. For my dad. You have to be eighteen or I'd do it myself. But I have money to pay his fee—all the money for my apartment in France. And then, once this is cleared up, it'll be like nothing happened. No trouble to you except going to the bail bondsman."

Already, he was shaking his head. "Tera, I'm sorry. You know I can't do that."

"But it's really easy. I'll give you the money. The woman on the phone said—"

"Not because of the money, or because it's too difficult. I can't get involved in this. It's not . . ." His eyes searched the room like he was looking for the right word. "Appropriate."

Something came between us then, sliding down and rattling shut. We weren't friends. We weren't mentor and favorite student. We weren't anything.

Heat pulsed from my cheeks. "I shouldn't have asked."

"I'm glad you trust me enough to—"

"I have to go. I'll be late."

He didn't try to stop me.

• • •

I spent most school lunch periods holed up in the girls' restroom on the second floor. I liked the quiet, the emptiness. I liked how no one could see me eating alone.

That day after my dad's arrest, the bathroom seemed colder, lonelier. I flipped open my phone and punched in the number for the jail. If Mr. Stewart wouldn't go to the bail bondsman, I'd have to find someone else.

I gave the woman on the phone my dad's booking number. "He was supposed to see the judge this morning." My voice echoed in the stillness of the bathroom. "I need to find out how much his bond is."

"Give me one minute."

I waited. This was a different woman from yesterday. This woman already sounded impatient.

"Okay, here it is. He was arraigned this morning." Computer keys clacked. "No bond."

A chill crawled up my arms. "What did you say?"

"Timothy H. Waters. It says right here, bond was denied."

"So I can't bail him out? That can't be right. Why would the judge do that?"

"Lots of reasons. He could be a flight risk. He could be a threat to civilians. But I don't know. If I knew, I'd have a bigger paycheck."

"But . . ." I tried to focus through a spreading haze. "I don't even know where he is, how to talk to him."

Her voice softened. "As of this morning, he's been moved to county. To the Samuel L. Mast facility. Here's the address."

I wrote it down. As long as I wrote, I didn't have to think.

"And here's the website." She rattled it off. "You can check it for visiting hours."

Easier said than done, since the police had my laptop. "What about a lawyer?" I asked. "Won't he get a lawyer?"

"The court appointed him counsel. You want the name? The counsel probably won't talk to you."

"Why wouldn't he talk to me?" But she didn't answer, just gave me the lawyer's name and number. She told me to have a nice day and hung up, and I leaned against the wall and stared at what I'd written.

For a few seconds, I couldn't move, couldn't think. Then the lawyer's number came into focus and I remembered Mom saying something about letting Dad's lawyer handle it. The lawyer would know what to do. I dialed the number, but an automated system kicked me over to his voice mail.

"You've reached Chase Hardy. Leave a brief message and a number where you can be reached."

"Um." I stumbled over my words. I should have planned what to say. "My name's Tera Waters. I'm the daughter of Timothy Waters. Who I guess you're helping? It's really important that you call me back because I think I know why he got arrested. I'm pretty sure it's my fault, so if you could call me back and tell me what's going on, I'd really appreciate it. I think I can help him." And then I left my number.

The bell rang. Lunch was over.

At the locker beside mine, Ian Walker cursed and pulled on his combination lock. It didn't open.

"It's fifteen, twenty-five, three," I reminded him. Our lockers had been beside each other's since freshman year, and he was always forgetting his combination.

"Thanks."

I felt his eyes on me as I dialed my own combination. I glanced over. Did he know?

He tried to smile, but it came out looking sad. "There's something you should see," he said.

"What is it?"

"Someone posted about you on the school forum. I don't even know who did it."

At first, I let myself hope that it had nothing to do with my dad. Maybe Mr. Stewart had made some announcement about my scholarship to the Paris Art Institute. I'd beat out hundreds of other applicants, so it was a pretty big deal.

But that had happened months ago. He wouldn't be posting about it now. This had to be about Dad.

"Can you show me?" I asked, already dreading what I'd see.

Ian pulled up the forum on his phone and scrolled down to a posting from RubyQueen15. "I don't know who this is," he said.

I didn't either. I could guess.

The post was short and sweet.

Everyone should know about this in case someone was planning on studying at Tera Waters's house.

And she was helpful enough to add a link: *BUSTED.com/illinois/decatur/timothy-h-waters.*

The post already had a few comments.

Sad. My heart goes out to Tera.

Stay strong girl.

So scary!!!

Whoever posted this should get a life. Who's monitoring this forum!?

Ian pointed to the last comment. "That one's from me."

I swallowed. "And the link?" I didn't want to see it, but I knew I had to.

Ian touched the screen. A man's face appeared. He looked like a typical thug. Blank stare. Expressionless mouth. Hair sticking up like razor wire. A mug shot of my dad.

And a caption to go with it.

3:27 P.M. March 12—Arrested: Timothy Henry Waters, 47, of Parker Lane, Decatur, Illinois. Charges: possession of child pornography.

Child pornography. Right there, for everyone to see.

Humiliation crawled up my back, clamped over my throat. I covered my face with my hands.

"It's okay," Ian said. "I'll make sure it gets taken down."

But it was too late. Now the link was out there. My own personal car wreck for everyone to rubberneck.

I felt naked, on display. All the kids in school would think I let my dad do things to me. They'd feel sorry for me. Tweet about me. Wonder what was wrong with me.

Ian kept talking, but nothing made sense. Some distant part of me heard shoes squeaking, lockers banging, shouting and talking and laughing. All of it so normal. All of it a strange fog I had to walk through to get to my next class.

CHAPTER 6

The Book

"No giggling, Tera." Her dad frowned from across the kitchen table. "If I see you giggling, it tells me you're not serious about this."

Tera clamped a hand over her mouth and tore her eyes away from the book. The book made her nervous, and she always giggled when she was nervous.

"It tells me you're not ready, that you're not old enough." He leaned back in his chair. "Is your mother right?"

She shook her head. Her ponytail whipped her shoulder. "I'm old enough."

"Then look at it. Tell me what you see."

"I see . . ." She felt a giggle coming, but she swallowed hard and it went away. "A book. I see an art book."

"Is that it?" He sounded disappointed.

"I see a book called Drawing Nudes."

"I didn't ask you to read the title." He pushed his chair back from the table like he was fed up. "I asked you, what do you see?"

"I see . . ." She squinted and pulled the book closer, knowing she had to give him the right answer so she'd be worth his time. It was one of those giant books with thick pages. It had a glossy cover, and on the cover was . . .

A naked woman, not covering herself at all. The woman's breasts made Tera want to cross her legs like she had to pee. She knew she was being stupid and immature. A real artist wouldn't feel weird like this. A real artist would see lines and curves and shades.

"I see beauty," she said.

Her dad snorted. "You're nine years old and you think the sight of a naked woman is beautiful? Not gross? Not intriguing? What the hell planet are you from?"

"But . . ." Sudden tears welled up behind her eyes. She'd told him what he wanted to hear, what a real artist would say.

"Listen, Tera, I'm not trying to trick you. I just want you to be honest and tell me what you see."

She swallowed hard to make the tears go away. "It makes me embarrassed," she whispered.

He nodded. "Now we're getting somewhere."

She went on, encouraged. "It makes me feel like I shouldn't be looking."

"Why?"

"Because she's naked."

He nodded his head like she'd said something important. "And that's what you need to get over. That uncomfortable feeling is what a girl your age who is not an artist would feel when she lays eyes on the naked human form."

She chanced a glance at his eyes, even though she was embarrassed to look at him with the naked woman between them. He wasn't looking at her, though. He was studying the naked lady like it was no big deal.

"Did you ever feel that way?" she asked.

"Embarrassed? Enthralled? Excited?" He laughed. "All of the above." Then he leaned back in his chair and smiled. "When I was in college I signed up for this class where we had live nude models. You know what that means?"

"Huh-uh."

"It means someone stood in front of our class and took their clothes off so we could draw them."

"Oh." She wondered if people really did that.

"And I was so . . ." He smiled like he was remembering something really good. "So fascinated, you might say, that I was distracted from doing my job. You know what my job was?"

"No."

"To learn. To learn everything I could about drawing the human form. Because once you get good at drawing nudes, it'll be easier to draw everything else."

"Like dogs?" Tera said. She loved drawing dogs but always had a hard time with their faces.

He chuckled. "I was thinking more along the lines of human faces, human torsos, hands, feet."

She found herself staring at the nude woman's body in a new way. Now she looked at the way the charcoal was smudged under the curves of her breasts. She noticed the feathering shades between the woman's legs.

"You get it, don't you? I see it on your face."

He was proud of her, she could tell. But she still felt shy. She laid her hand on the book so it covered the woman's body. "It's for me?"

"Who else?" He winked at her. "And I have a surprise for you." He craned his neck to look out the window behind her. She turned to see what he was looking at, but it was only a car going by.

"A surprise? Do I get to guess what it is?"

"You can try, but you'll never guess."

"Tell me," she said. "Please."

His eyes strayed back to the window for a moment. "You have to keep it to yourself. It's a secret."

Tera knew all about keeping secrets. Just last week she and Haley had watched a dirty movie that Haley found buried in her dad's sock drawer. Haley made Tera promise not to tell anyone. Like Tera would ever in a billion years say what those people had been doing to each other. She couldn't even think about it without feeling excited and weird and ashamed.

"Did you hear what I said? You can't tell anyone—not your friends, not your teachers, not your mom."

Tera nodded. "I promise."

He tilted his head to look at her. "You won't see the value of it, not until later. But it is valuable."

"Tell me."

"I'm building it up too much. You'll be disappointed when I tell you."

"I won't be."

He placed his hands flat on the table. "I made arrangements for you to sketch your first nude model. Next week."

Her smile froze. "You mean a real person?" A real naked *person. Already her heart felt jumpy. There was no way she could draw someone naked. One time at Burger King, she walked in on a lady going to the bathroom, and even though the lady said it was okay, Tera ran away crying with her hands covering her eyes.*

"I went to a lot of trouble to arrange this." Her dad reached across the table and took her chin in his hand. "Look at me. You know what I see?"

She tried to shake her head, but he was holding her too tightly.

"You're supposed to say, 'Yes,'" he said. "You're supposed to know what I see when I look at you. I'll give you a hint. Do I see a girly-girl who's too busy playing with dolls to become a serious artist?"

"No," she whispered, even though she still liked playing Barbies.

"Do I see a loud-mouthed tattletale who's going to tell all her friends that she's learning to draw naked people?"

"No." She knew better than to tell her friends, especially Haley, who had a big mouth.

"Do I see a budding young artist? A protégé? A young lady who's serious enough to handle what many people in their twenties aren't ready for?"

She knew she was supposed to say yes and when she hesitated, she saw his eyes flicker like he was getting fed up. "Yes," she said.

He smiled and let go of her chin, tugging on her ponytail. "Good girl."

But then his smile disappeared, wiped from his face. He stared out the window behind her, his eyes scared. A second later she heard a car rattling down the driveway.

"Mom's home," he said, which wasn't scary at all, but the way he scuttled to his feet with his head whipping toward the door made her feel like she should run and hide. He swept the book off the table and shoved it at her chest so hard that she stumbled backward.

Then he snarled at her. "What the hell are you waiting for?"

"I don't know." She tried not to cry as the key rattled in the lock.

"Hide the goddamn book," he hissed. "Hide it where she won't find it."

CHAPTER 7

My high school wasn't that big, so it didn't take long for everyone in the building to hear about my dad. No one said anything, but I could see it in their faces, the way their eyes slid away as they huddled at their lockers, the way conversations stopped when I approached. In AP Biology, everyone kept turning around to look at me, so by the time class was over I felt like a specimen in one of Mr. Rudolph's glass jars.

World History was next, the class I dreaded most because I shared it with Haley. The less time I had to spend in the same room with her, the better, so before class started I stopped at the library to borrow one of the school's laptops.

As soon as I stepped into the library, a peaceful quiet surrounded me. I stood in the doorway for a few seconds, listening to the hum of silence, breathing in the smell of books, wishing I could hide among the tall shelves for the rest of the day.

I didn't see anybody except for Mrs. Sloan, the tall, willowy librarian. She sat behind her desk sorting books from the return bin into wobbly stacks. She glanced up from her work and smiled. "How are you, Tera? Reading anything good these days?"

I shrugged. "Not really."

"Well, then, I have some recommendations for you."

I tried to sound casual as I approached her desk. If she hadn't heard the rumors about my dad, I didn't want to tip her off that something was wrong. "I didn't really come here to check out a book," I said. "I wanted to see if we're allowed to borrow school laptops. To check out, I mean."

"Yes, of course."

"Mine got stolen," I adding, knowing I was giving too much information. Wasn't that the first sign of a lie?

"I'm sorry to hear that." She pushed her chair back from her desk. "It'll take me a few minutes to get it checked out for you. Do you want to swing by after school and pick it up? I don't want you to be late for class."

Up until that moment, I had every intention of finishing out the school day, but then it occurred to me that, if I cut class, I wouldn't have to deal with Haley. Instead of sitting through World History, I could go to the public library with the laptop and learn all I could about child pornography charges without Mom sticking her nose in.

"I'm not worried about being late," I said. "I have permission to leave."

"Oh." She should have asked me to show some kind of note from a teacher to prove I was telling the truth, but that's one of the perks of being a good student. Teachers don't expect you to lie through your teeth. They don't expect you to skip class.

A few minutes later, she handed me the laptop and all its cords. "Sorry I don't have a carrying case," she said.

"That's okay." I shoved the laptop into my backpack. "Thanks."

From there, it was easy to walk out the front door of the school.

● ● ●

I sat in one of the private computer cubicles at the public library and searched the Internet for how to help my dad.

The more I learned, the more hopeless it all seemed.

One of the first things I read was how anyone found guilty of possessing child pornography would get *at least* five years in prison. So that drawing I did all those years ago could cost my dad five years of his life.

And then I read how the other prisoners preyed on anyone convicted of a sexual crime against children. In their eyes, that person was the lowest of the low. I read about a case in Omaha where the inmates actually killed a priest who was serving time for child molestation.

And then I read something that scared me even more.

In cases like my dad's—cases that involved just the *accusation* of child pornography without any real proof—most lawyers told their clients to plead guilty in exchange for less prison time. The article said juries almost always gave a guilty verdict to anyone being accused of a sexual crime against children. Most lawyers felt child pornography cases were such a lost cause that they didn't even try to help their clients unless they were paying them big money.

My dad wasn't paying his lawyer anything. The courts appointed him. That meant there was a good chance Chase Hardy would tell my dad to plead guilty just to get the case off his books.

I had to talk to Dad's lawyer. I had to explain to him that I was the one who did the drawing. Once he knew all the facts, my dad's case should be easy. They might even drop the charges and Dad could come home and everything would go back to normal.

● ● ●

I learned one other important thing from my Internet research. Prisoners had to call collect to reach the outside world. And since my cell phone didn't accept collect calls, Dad would have to call the house if he wanted to talk to me. That meant he had to get past Mom's defenses. She had a habit of taking the phone off the hook when she wanted to hide from the world. And if she answered the phone before I could get to it, there was no way she'd let me talk to him.

The first thing I did when I got home was check the phone in the kitchen to make sure it had a dial tone. It did. Then I checked to make sure Mom was in her bedroom. She was.

After that, I went to my room and shut the door. While I started up my borrowed laptop, I tried calling Dad's lawyer again on my cell phone. The house phone rang before I could finish dialing.

I jumped up. It could be Dad. I had to answer it before Mom got to it.

Another ring. I made a dash for the kitchen, but then it stopped. Shit. I heard Mom's voice from her bedroom, sounding bone-tired as she answered it. I picked up the phone in the kitchen and listened.

". . . don't call here again," Mom was saying.

Then my dad. "I just want to talk to her, Connie."

I practically screamed into the phone. "Dad, it's me!"

"Tera! I don't—"

And then nothing. A chasm of silence. She must have unplugged the phone.

I slammed down the receiver, so angry I wanted to break it. "Mom!" My voice bounced against the walls as I stormed down the hallway. I burst into her room. The loose phone cord dangled from her fist. "What is your problem?" I yelled.

She didn't even blink. Her mouth was set in a smug line. "The school called. They said you skipped class."

Of course, she would try to change the subject. I grabbed the phone cord out of her hand and threw it on the bed. "Why won't you let me talk to him? It's not hurting you to let me talk to him."

My yelling didn't seem to faze her. She pulled at a loose string on the blanket like it was the most important thing on the planet. "They're not giving you a detention this time," she said, "but don't expect them to be lenient in the future."

"Will you shut up for a second? He's all alone in there. Don't you get that? He needs to know I'm here, that I haven't given up on him."

"There's nothing you can do for him, Tera."

"That's not true!"

She stopped fiddling with the blanket long enough to stare me in the face. "I'm trying to help you and you won't let me. Always, since you were a little girl, you've taken his side. Why is that?" Her laugh sounded limp and hollow as she pulled the blanket onto her lap. "Never mind. I don't want to know."

"Of course you don't. All you want to do is torture me. All you want to do is ruin my life."

"That's not true, and you know it."

"It *is* true, Mom. I'm so sick of you. Sometimes I hate you."

I stayed long enough to see the hurt on her face. Then I left the room, slamming the door behind me. Guilt bit at me—I shouldn't have said I hated her—but I told myself not to feel bad. Let her sit there and wallow in her sweaty sheets. She didn't want me, and I didn't need her.

Back in my room, I dialed Dad's lawyer.

This time he answered, snapping out his name like a rubber band. "Chase Hardy here."

"Um, hi." My heart was pounding. I scooted to the edge of my bed. "This is Tera Waters. I'm the daughter of Tim—"

"Yeah, I know who you are."

"Okay." My voice shook. I tried to hold it steady so I didn't sound like a stupid kid. "I wanted to tell you about why my dad is innocent. The police found that drawing of the girl, but he didn't do it. I did."

I waited for his reaction—I pictured him sitting up straighter in his chair, grabbing a pen to make sure he didn't miss anything—but all I could hear was a woman's voice in the background, a phone ringing.

Maybe the reception was bad. "Hello?" I said. "Can you hear me?"

"Is that why you keep calling?" His voice was cold and flat, like what I was telling him wasn't the least bit important.

Which meant the police must have found the photo.

Which meant Dad could be in a lot of trouble. Five years in prison. The other prisoners beating the crap out of him, maybe even killing him.

I had to tell this lawyer everything, get it out in the open.

"There was a photo, too," I said. "But it's not what you think."

"No, I imagine not."

"It's kind of a long story. I can tell you on the phone, or I can come to your office. I can come now if you want, or I can—"

"Miss Waters, let me stop you right there."

I clamped my mouth shut. This was where he'd tell me how everything would be okay. I *so* wanted to hear him tell me everything would be okay.

"If you're really concerned about your father's welfare, the best thing you can do is let me handle this."

He sounded like he was done talking, but I needed more. "I wanted to make sure you knew everything," I said. "How the photo wasn't a big deal. So you don't have to have him plead guilty or anything because he's actually really innocent."

"I have to go."

"Wait!" That couldn't be it. If he hung up, I'd lose my only connection to what was going on. I tried to sound forceful, grown up. "I need to know how you're going to help him."

"Did no one explain this to you?" Chase Hardy spoke slowly, like he was talking down to a child. "I cannot share with you— nor would I want to—the details of your father's case."

"But I know how these things work. You won't have him plead guilty, right?"

"Frankly, it's none of your business what my client and I decide."

Why was he pushing me away? All I was doing was trying to help.

He wasn't done. "And for you to tell me how I should handle his case is exactly why I can't deal with family members."

"But I'm his *daughter.*" By that time, I was almost crying. "I have a right to be involved."

"I don't have time for this. You cannot imagine how busy I am. And the more time I spend communicating with frantic family members, the less time I have to defend my clients. Do you understand what I'm telling you?"

He didn't wait for me to answer. He hung up.

I sat there on my bed, stunned, staring at the phone in my hand. Everything I had read about court-appointed attorneys was true. He had no interest in helping my dad.

All that research I'd done. Everyone said the same thing. If you wanted to clear your name of child pornography charges, you needed to hire a lawyer who specialized in sex crimes.

And if I hired a sex crimes lawyer for my dad, I wouldn't be going to France.

CHAPTER 8

Fact one: The judge was not letting my dad out on bail.

Fact two: Mom was useless—more than useless, since she was basically fighting for the other side.

Fact three: Chase Hardy had no interest in getting to the truth. He wasn't going to fight for my dad.

And fact four: If I paid for a lawyer, I wouldn't have enough money for an apartment in France. Maybe not even enough for a plane ticket.

My scholarship to the Paris Art Institute paid my tuition for an entire year, but there were no dorms attached to the college. I had to live in an apartment, off campus, and that meant my living expenses weren't covered by financial aid. I already had an apartment lined up, just four blocks from the school and six blocks from the Louvre. If I did this for my dad, there was no way I could afford to go. Not this year, at least.

But I had to help him. He needed a good lawyer to stay out of prison. If he went to prison, the other inmates would beat him, maybe even kill him.

So in a way, my decision was easy.

The art institute's website said that, under special circumstances, you could postpone using your scholarship money. So there was no reason not to help him. And after I broke the plan into steps, it didn't seem that complicated. First, I'd get a deferment on my scholarship so I could use it next year. Second, I'd pay for a lawyer out of my Paris fund. Third, I'd get back my old job at Papa Geppetto's. And finally, after I saved enough for an apartment in Paris, I'd reinstate my scholarship. The last step would be easy, but I had a long way to go.

I spent an hour crafting an e-mail to the art institute's financial aid department, formally requesting a deferment on my scholarship. I stressed over the wording and made sure to include all the information they requested.

Step two was more complicated. I had to learn all I could about lawyers.

What to look for in a good lawyer. What kinds of questions to ask. How long the whole process might take. I found out that lawyers want to be paid up front—a retainer, they called it—and the retainer could run anywhere from ten to thirty thousand dollars. If my dad's case dragged on, I might need more than the twenty thousand dollars I had in my account. I needed to start working right away.

Just typing the words *sex crimes attorneys* into the browser felt sleazy, but at least my dad wasn't alone. Going by the number of attorneys who specialized in sex crimes, I thought there must be a sexual predator lurking around every corner. I liked how all the lawyers acted like getting arrested for rape or child pornography could happen to anyone. Maybe it could.

All the attorneys' webpages said the same thing. People got frantic when it came to child pornography charges. It didn't matter if the charges were bogus. The tiniest suspicion could trigger a witch hunt. And the longer you waited to hire a specialized lawyer, the greater your chance of being burned at the stake.

I felt time slipping away. A full day had passed since Dad's arrest. Everything I read said the other side was already hard at work, building a case against him.

I picked up my phone to call the first lawyer on my list. Then I noticed how my room had grown dark. No lawyer would be in the office on a Friday night. I'd have to wait. I turned off the light and tried to sleep.

Before all this happened, I used to lie in bed and think about art school and what it would be like to live in Paris. But that night, all I could think about was my dad in his jail cell. Sitting on a bare cot, his head in his hands. Pacing his cage, trying to figure out what had happened. Closing his eyes in that empty darkness, hoping to sleep, waiting for someone to rescue him.

• • •

The next morning, I stayed in bed and let myself pretend it was all a dream—that my dad had never gotten arrested, that I was still going to the Paris Art Institute. I let myself imagine the scenario I'd played over and over in my head, before any of this happened. Me sitting up late in my apartment, talking with my classmates about colors and technique, about professors and boys. Only now the imagining wasn't fun anymore. Pretending hurt too much. And I didn't have time for that anyway. I had to find my dad a lawyer.

I dragged myself out of bed and started calling the lawyers on my list, but none of them picked up. One of them had a voice-mail message that said to call back Monday during regular office hours. That's when I figured out lawyers don't work on Saturday.

I closed my eyes, frustrated. Already it had been two days since Dad's arrest. If I waited till Monday, the lawyer going against Dad would have a four-day head start.

Time to try something else. I pulled the computer onto my lap and typed, *24-7 sex crime attorneys, Decatur, Illinois.*

Most of the links were junk, but one stood out. When I clicked on it, the words *Do Not Panic and Do Not Lose Hope!* marched across the top of the page. I kept reading.

If you have been accused of a sex crime, you are no doubt wondering how anyone could believe such outrageous allegations. You probably feel frustrated that the police are not being objective when looking at the so-called evidence. You may question why the authorities seem intent on convicting you without a full investigation. Undoubtedly, you feel frightened, discouraged, and alone.

That sounded exactly like what my dad was going through. When I scrolled down, I saw they offered free consultations. Their office was open twenty-four hours a day, seven days a week.

I swept up my phone and punched in the number. A woman answered after the first ring.

"David A. Kaufmann and Associates. This is Linda. How may I help you?"

"Um, hi. I'm looking for a lawyer. For my dad, not me."

"What's he charged with, honey?"

"I guess it would be . . ." I rubbed the back of my neck. "Pornography." I couldn't bring myself to say *child* pornography.

"Well, you called the right place."

I felt my shoulders relax a little. Someone was going to help me. Someone was going to help my dad. "I'm not sure how this works," I said. "I think I have enough money to get started. And I guess I have to meet with him? The lawyer, I mean."

"I'll set up a consultation. But you do understand. It wouldn't be *you* hiring the attorney. Your father would do the actual hiring."

"But I'm the one with the money," I said.

"I understand, but you'd only be acting as your father's agent. Would you like to set up a consultation?"

"Can I see the lawyer today?"

"Of course. How's eleven o'clock?"

"Perfect."

I almost smiled when I hung up. Finally, things were happening.

● ● ●

I stepped off the bus and checked my hand where I'd scribbled the lawyer's address. Was I even in the right place? These were houses, not office buildings, and most of them looked rundown with their peeling paint and broken shutters. Then I saw a blue BMW parked in one of the driveways. That house had a fresh paint job, decorative stones lining the walkway, bushes shaped like perfect rectangles. Above the door was a plaque: *The Law Offices of David A. Kaufmann & Associates.*

For a split second, I wanted to forget about the whole thing. Go to Paris and let my dad deal with his own problems. But I knew I couldn't do that. Even if I hated this lawyer, I'd keep searching until I found someone else.

Inside, the office looked empty, but I heard a copier going, and I smelled burned popcorn. I stepped up to the front desk and craned my neck to see around a bookshelf. A blonde woman in a gray pantsuit stood at the copier.

"Excuse me," I said.

She looked up, smiling when she saw me. "Can I help you?"

"I'm Tera Waters. I have an appointment?"

"Yes, we spoke on the phone. I'm Linda." She pushed up her sleeve and glanced at her watch. "You're a little early, but I think Ms. Gross can see you now."

She led me through a door to where a woman sat behind a big wooden desk, typing on her computer. She looked about my mom's age and wore a navy blue pantsuit with a string of pearls around her neck. Her hair was up in a bun.

Linda introduced us. "Ms. Gross, this is Tera Waters. Ms. Waters, this is Charlotte Gross, senior criminal defense attorney."

I shook her hand. She had a French manicure. She probably had her nails done every week.

Linda left the room, and the lawyer pointed to one of the cushioned chairs that faced her desk. "Have a seat. May I call you Tera?"

I nodded and sat, clenching my purse. Through the fake leather, I could feel my checkbook.

"Can you tell me what happened?" she asked.

I had to clear my throat to get the words out. "The police arrested my dad."

"And the charges? Did you hear why they arrested him?"

My fingers ached from gripping my purse so hard. I didn't want to say it, but I knew I had to. "For child pornography."

I waited for the shocked pause, the gasp. But she didn't flinch, didn't even blink.

"But I know he's innocent," I said.

"And what makes you say that?"

"The police found a drawing, but I'm the one who did it, not him."

"A drawing? I don't understand."

"He's an artist. We both are. I did a drawing of myself when I was a kid. I was just practicing—you know, drawing the nude form. But I guess it could be considered pornographic."

I checked her face, but all I saw was concern. "You were there when they searched the house?" she asked. "Did they have a warrant, or did someone let them in?"

"They had a warrant, but I let them in. I'm pretty sure my mom called them."

She made a note on her pad. "Did you see what they took?"

"His computer. My laptop. Some folders with a bunch of his sketches."

"And why do you think they took all that?"

"Because . . ." I clenched my jaw. This was where I had to say it. "Because there was a photo of me," I blurted. "At least I think there was. A digital photo. Mom said she found something on his computer. That's why she called them. So the police must have found the photo, too, on his computer, and then they took his hard drive and a bunch of other stuff hoping they'd find something else." I rambled on, wanting her to stop me, but she was taking notes on her pad. "I think they were fishing because it's *not* a big deal. The photo, I mean. Or the drawing. That's what the police do, right? They fish. And you can't explain anything to my mom. There's something wrong with her. She takes medication for depression and anxiety. That's important, right?"

"It could be." She scribbled something else on her pad. "But I need you to back up a little."

"Okay." I thought for sure she wanted to talk about the photo. Why was I in it? Why did he have it? But that's not what she asked.

"How old were you when you did the drawing?"

"Nine, I think."

"And how old are you now?"

"Seventeen. Almost eighteen."

She nodded, wrote something on her pad. "And you were nine years old in the photo?"

"Yes." I waited for her to finish writing. "Can you help him? *Will* you help him?"

She leaned back in her chair. "You understand that nothing is a sure thing."

"I understand."

"But I'm sure we can resolve this so it makes sense. Whatever tack I take, I want you to feel confident that your dad is making a good decision."

"Okay."

She tapped her pen against her chin. "Do you want to talk money now?"

"Yes." My stomach tightened. What if I didn't have enough?

"This is a felony charge. You understand that, right?"

I nodded.

"In this type of case, my retainer would be eighteen thousand dollars. If the case goes to trial, that amount would increase significantly."

I actually breathed a sigh of relief. I had enough. I'd even have two thousand dollars left over to start up my Paris fund again.

"Okay," I said. "I can do that."

"You need to be sure, Tera. If your father changes his mind—if *you* change your mind—the money is still spent."

I'd already made my decision. I was Dad's only hope, and I had to do this. "I understand," I said. I pulled out my checkbook.

"Your dad has to agree. He has to sign the papers."

"I know."

She handed me a pen, one of those fancy designer ones, heavy in my hand. "I won't cash your check until we have your father's signature."

I'd written only one other check in my life—for the application fee to the Paris Art Institute—and it wasn't anywhere near eighteen thousand dollars. I remembered how I felt when I wrote that check. Excited and hopeful. I knew I should feel hopeful writing this check, too. I was saving my dad. But to do it, I was giving up the thing that had kept me going for so long. The one thing I looked forward to when I woke up in the morning.

My hand started to shake as I wrote the amount, so I tried to pretend I was painting. The fancy pen seemed to call for big, flowery letters, and when I got to the last part, the part where I signed my name, I used fast, flourished strokes, like I was signing my name to a work of art.

I thought my dad would like that.

CHAPTER 9

Humpty Dumpty

Tera huddled on the couch, her hands pressed to her ears. It didn't help. She could still hear them fighting in their bedroom.

"*What were you thinking?*" Her mom's voice. Shrieky. "*She's only nine years old!*"

They were fighting about her. Mostly her mom did all the yelling, but her dad had a way of saying things that dug in deep and hurt for a long time.

"*. . . mature for her age,*" he was saying. "*. . . more talent than . . .*"

Tera uncovered her ears and sat very still. He sounded proud of her. She moved off the couch and crept her way up the hallway, stopping outside their bedroom. Shadows flashed beneath the door.

"*. . . can't believe you think this is okay.*" Her mom's voice, still loud. "*What else are you teaching her?*"

Her dad laughed. "*You should see yourself, Connie. I can't believe you're getting this worked up over a nude model.*"

"*She's too young! There's something wrong with you if you don't see that.*"

"*If you were an artist, or bothered to know anything about what your daughter is interested in, you'd know it's not a big deal.*"

"*It* is *a big deal. You're turning her into your little disciple. And she won't listen to me because you tell her I'm crazy.*"

He laughed again. "*I don't have to tell her that.*"

"*Fuck you, Tim!*"

Tera flinched as the door flew open and her mom barreled out of the room. Her mom almost walked into her before she looked down.

Disgust, plain on her face. She had a book under her arm. The Drawing Nudes *book. She must have found it under Tera's bed.*

Almost, it felt good to not have the secret anymore. Some secrets were fun, but this one didn't feel right.

"It's just the human form, Connie." Her dad called. He was lounging on the bed. "You're turning it into something dirty, and it's not."

"Then why was she hiding it?" She shoved the book at Tera's face. "If it's just a book, why were you hiding it?"

Tera swallowed. "Dad said—"

Her dad interrupted. "Because she knew you'd act like a lunatic if you saw it."

"Did he tell you to hide it?"

Dad wouldn't want her to tell the truth, but she always got caught when she lied. Instead of answering, she stared at her mom's feet. The Drawing Nudes *book had a whole section on drawing feet. Maybe she should tell her mom that.*

"He did, didn't he? He told you to hide it."

Tera looked up. Her mom held the book, her fingertips touching the woman's breasts. Tera dropped her eyes to the floor, embarrassed.

"You can't look at it, can you? Well, now you don't have to." And then she tore off the dust cover and ripped it into pieces. The pieces scattered at Tera's feet.

Her dad watched the whole thing from the bed, shaking his head and laughing. "Unbelievable," he said.

Tera imagined she was a turtle pulling herself into her shell. She put her head down, scrunched in her arms and legs.

But her mom wouldn't let her hide. "Do you understand how wrong this is?" She grabbed her arm and yanked her up. "Do you?"

Tera's teeth rattled as her mom shook her. She tried to talk, but she didn't know the right answer.

"Leave her alone, Connie." Her dad's voice. Quiet and calm. "You're the one turning this into something."

Tera snuck a look at her mom's face. Her eyes were closed, her forehead wrinkled, like she was thinking really hard. She gave Tera's arm a shake, and Tera almost cried out because her mom's fingernails were so sharp. Then her mom let go and stomped away.

She rubbed the red marks on her arm. Her dad came up beside her. "You okay?"

She looked at the ripped paper scattered at her feet and thought of Humpty Dumpty. All the king's horses and all the king's men . . .

"I'm okay," she said.

Her dad put his hand on her chin and lifted her face. Checking for tears, maybe.

Tera made herself smile, glad her eyes weren't wet. Nothing to give her away. Dad didn't like it when she acted sad.

CHAPTER 10

As soon as I walked in the door to Papa Geppetto's Pizzeria, the yeasty odor of rising dough brought back all the bad memories of working there. How the smell stayed trapped in my hair and skin. How I'd scurry around trying to make everyone happy and still have customers yell at me because I wasn't fast enough.

I stood by the counter and looked around. The restaurant was empty. No customers. No employees that I could see. The lunch rush had ended, but the dining room was still a mess. Straw wrappers and spilled Parmesan all over the green carpet. Tables stacked with dirty dishes. Dressing and sesame seeds splattering the salad bar.

Footsteps echoed behind me in the stillness. I turned to see a guy coming around the corner from the kitchen, a guy about my age, with tousled sun-brown hair and dark lashes. He had a lazy, confident walk. He looked like the type who could date any girl he wanted.

Which meant he'd want nothing to do with me.

He stopped when he saw me, like I was some kind of surprise. Slowly, his eyes scanned my body, a cat's tongue on my skin. My neck tingled.

"Is it just you?" he asked.

For a second, I didn't know what he meant. "No," I said. "I mean, yes. It's just me. But I didn't come here for a table. I'm looking for a job."

He had beautiful eyes. Hazel, flecked with green and yellow. I read his nametag. *Joey.* "So you need an application?" he asked.

"No, that's okay." I was glad I had a reason to stand there. Otherwise, I might have turned and run. "Is Mr. Barnes still manager?" I asked.

His smile reminded me of a fox. "You mean Dick?"

"Um, I think he goes by Richard."

Joey leaned across the counter, close enough for me to smell the mint on his breath. "I think he likes Dick better."

I blinked and drew back. Was that a slam at Mr. Barnes for being gay? "Maybe I'll just call him Mr. Barnes," I said.

"Probably smart." Joey studied me. "So you know him?"

"I used to work here."

"Then you know he's a cool guy."

"Yeah, I know." I scratched my arm. So, not gay bashing?

"Don't move," he said. "I'll go get him."

I made a point of *not* following him with my eyes. Guys like him expected girls like me to watch them. Instead I grabbed a take-out menu off the counter and stared at it. A minute passed. Then I heard voices from the back room, drawing nearer.

"I didn't get her name," Joey was saying. "You want me to tell you what she looks like?"

"Never mind, Joey. I'll see her in a second."

Joey grinned at me as he came around the corner. Again, his eyes moved over me, slower this time. I stood there like a statue in a museum. Part of me wanted to cross my arms over my chest. Another part wanted to straighten my spine.

Mr. Barnes held his arms out. "Tera Waters! I thought maybe it was you."

"Hi, Mr. Barnes." I glanced at Joey. Still staring. "You said I could come back anytime I needed a job?"

"I did say that." Mr. Barnes made a shooing motion to Joey. "Go finish the dough. And then do something about that salad bar."

Joey pushed himself off the counter. A lazy ripple. "Yes, Mr. Barnes. Sir." His eyes caught mine. I glanced away.

"I can start whenever you need me," I said.

"How about this week? One of my waitresses quit."

"Yeah, sure." I watched Joey disappear around the corner. "I'm still in school, but I can do the dinner shift."

"Perfect. Let me go get the paperwork."

So I had a job. I'd either use the money to keep paying the lawyer, or I'd put it in the bank so I could go to France next year.

Mr. Barnes came back with the tax forms, and I sat in one of the booths to fill them out. I could hear Joey singing an old Beatles song in the back room. "I Want to Hold Your Hand." His voice was good. Maybe he was in a band. I could picture him playing guitar.

Mr. Barnes returned after a few minutes. "If you're finished, you can come back to my office and I'll put you on the schedule."

I grabbed my purse and followed him past the prep table to his tiny office at the end of the corridor. No Joey in sight.

Mr. Barnes took the schedule off the wall and laid it on his desk. He picked up a pencil. "What days *can't* you work?"

I scanned the schedule for Joey's name. He worked the evening shift on Monday and Tuesday. "I'm free all week," I said. "Any evening you need me."

"Let's see. Sadie's working on Monday. She can retrain you. How about Monday, Thursday, and Saturday?"

So only one day with Joey. "Okay."

Somewhere down the hall, Joey was singing again. I watched for him as I made my way back to the front. I didn't see him, but I told myself it didn't matter. He'd never go for someone like me. No one ever went for me. Dad said it was because I intimidated them. Dad said a lot of things.

Dad. And suddenly it hit me again, the ugly truth spreading like a mushroom cloud. *My dad is in jail.*

A head rush clouded my vision, made me hang on to the door. Probably at that moment Dad was sitting on a lumpy cot staring at steel bars, thinking how alone he was, how everyone in his life had ditched him. And here I was getting distracted by some guy who I imagined was flirting with me, who probably forgot about me the second I left his sight. Guilt weighed on my shoulders.

I'm trying, Dad.

I was halfway out the door when Joey's voice called me.

"Hey, Tera! Wait!"

I froze, turned. Joey sauntered toward me. He had something under his arm. My purse. I *never* forgot my purse.

He stopped and held it out. My hand closed around it, but he didn't let go. Our fingertips touched. Our eyes locked. And something stirred inside me. Something physical and deep.

"Thanks," I heard myself say.

He let go. I could have taken a step back, but I didn't. "You should be more careful," he said.

I groped for something to say, but all my words got snagged in a swirl of emotions. Only one thing to do. I lowered my eyes, clutched my purse, and started walking.

"See you Monday," he called.

I turned. He waved. I think I waved back.

I don't remember crossing the parking lot or walking down the sidewalk. I don't remember the clouds or the rain or the puddles. Only when I was under the shelter of the bus stop did I realize I was soaking wet and that Joey knew what day I was working. I wasn't sure if that meant anything, but as I rode the bus home, I caught myself *not* thinking about Dad again. This time I had to work harder to make myself feel guilty.

● ● ●

Mom sat on the couch like a lump of dirty laundry. She wore the same faded t-shirt and torn sweatpants she'd slept in. *Dr. Phil* blasted on the television.

"Where were you?" she asked. "You've been gone all day."

I almost lied to her, but what was the point? She'd find out eventually. I took a seat on the edge of the couch. "I got a job."

"That's good." Her eyes never left the television. "I was going to do that, too."

"Get a job? Really?"

She lowered the volume on the television but didn't turn it off. "Now that your dad's gone, we'll have to pull together."

Like we were a team. Like Dad was never coming back. "It's not like he's dead," I said.

"He's dead to me."

The way she said it, her voice flat, almost sad, as though Dad had really died. Grief bit at me. "You're being stupid," I snapped. "He'll be out of there soon and then you'll see how stupid you're being."

"Funny." She reached for the afghan on the back of the couch and pulled it onto her lap. "I was thinking the same about you."

Her words dug in like barbs. I wanted to rip them out and throw them at her.

"I didn't get a job to help *you*," I said. "You're the one who called the police. You're the reason he's in jail."

"Here you go again." Her eyelids fluttered. "Always taking his side."

"I got the job because I hired a lawyer," I said. "And the lawyer's expensive."

I waited for a reaction, but she seemed engrossed in *Dr. Phil.*

"So I won't be going to Paris in the fall," I said.

That got a reaction. A muscle in her cheek twitched. "What about your scholarship?"

"I asked for a deferral."

"What does that mean?"

"If they say yes, then my scholarship will still be good for next year."

"And what if they say no?"

"I don't know, Mom. They won't say no. The website said they offer deferrals for up to two years."

She curled her hands into the afghan and lifted it to her chest. "I suppose you want me to congratulate you? Because you threw away your future?"

"I didn't throw it away. I'll still go, just not in the fall. And I'm helping my dad. That's what family does."

"That's a sweet sentiment, Tera. But you're helping the wrong person."

Anger made my chest hurt. It was her vindictiveness that had caused this whole thing. "You wanted me to give the money to you, didn't you? You thought you'd get rid of Dad, and you'd still be okay because I'd give up my trip to France to help out with the bills."

"That's not true."

"Well, it's my money," I said. "It's my de—"

"It's your decision, I know. And you're almost an adult. So there's nothing I can do to stop you." Finally, she turned her head to look at me. "Is that what you were going to say?"

It was, but I kept my mouth shut.

She sighed and went back to watching television. "Just go away, Tera."

The loathing in her words snuck into my chest and settled there, taking up space. She didn't want to be around me. I wasn't worth her time. I sat, wanting her to look at me. Yell at me. Anything.

Not even an eye flicker, but that was okay. She wasn't arguing with me. I didn't have to listen to her yelling. Maybe she didn't realize I'd won, but I had.

My victory felt fragile, though, so I got up from the couch as quiet as a ghost and edged my way out of her sight.

CHAPTER 11

A Secret

Tera's mom and dad waited at the kitchen table, her mom's face like a rock, her dad tilting his chair on two legs. Something was wrong. She'd done something wrong.

"Sit down," her dad said. A lit cigarette rested in the ashtray, the ash so long it looked like a finger.

She shrank into the empty chair between them. Her mom pulled something off her lap and smacked it on the table. Tera's sketchpad of good paper, the one her dad had given to her for her birthday. She'd printed her name on the cover in black marker: Tera Waters, age 9. *So far it only had one drawing because she'd thrown all the others away. She should have thrown this one away, too, but she'd saved it to show her dad. She thought it was good, maybe the best she'd ever done. But that didn't matter. She should have thrown it away.*

Her mom flipped open the sketchpad, and there it was, the one drawing. A naked girl. Haley. Draped over the couch like Rose from the Titanic *movie. Just like Rose when Jack sketched her in the nude.*

Haley lay on her side, her head propped on her arm. Her other hand touched her forehead, just like Rose. And Haley wore a necklace, but Haley's was a little heart, a lot smaller than Rose's blue diamond. Haley's breasts were smaller, too, not a woman's breasts at all, no matter what Haley said.

Her dad tilted forward. His chair thumped to the floor. Her mom leaned forward, too. They all stared at the drawing in painful silence. Tera was afraid to breathe.

Then her mom spoke: "Who did this? Tell me the truth."

She almost said Haley did it, but they all knew Haley couldn't draw. Tera chanced a look at her dad. His eyes were on the drawing. She couldn't tell if he thought it was good or not. "I did it," she said.

A quick breath from her mom, her voice low. "Did he tell you to do it?"

"No."

"Don't lie to me."

"I'm not lying."

"I tried to tell you, Connie." Her dad was using his high-and-mighty voice.

But Mom was sick of him, sick of Tera, too. She ripped out the drawing and shoved it in Tera's face. "Why would you draw this? Why would you do this to your best friend?"

Tera blinked and ducked, like the sketch was a weapon and not a flimsy piece of paper. "It was her idea," Tera said. It felt like tattling, but she didn't want her mom thinking bad things about her.

Her dad's eyebrows went up. "You showed this to Haley?"

"She posed for it," Tera said. "We were just . . . I wanted to practice and she said she'd pose for me. We watched Titanic *when she spent the night and she wanted to be Rose. She wanted me to turn her into Rose."*

"So not a big deal," her dad said. "Just like I told you." He put a fresh cigarette between his lips, paused before lighting it to wink at Tera. Like they were a team. A team against Mom.

"Give me that." Her mom swiped the lighter out of his hand. She held the sketch by one corner and lit a flame. The flame licked at the sketch. The sketch burned. First Haley's hair, then her eyes, her pretty mouth. The necklace with its little heart. And then the rest of her. Her whole body veiled in fire and then gone. The burning smelled good. A lot better than her dad's cigarettes.

Her mom walked to the sink, turned on the faucet, held the burning paper under the water. The fire went out with a sizzle of smoke. She tossed the soggy wad of paper in the trash. "Go to your room," she told Tera. "Get rid of all the filthy pictures I know you've done. Because if I find another one, I'll burn up everything you have. All your paper, your pencils, your paint. Just to keep you from doing this. Do you understand me?"

"Yes," Tera whispered. Her mom looked crazy, her face tight, her pinched eyes shining black.

"Don't make me do it!" Her mom glared at the lighter in her hand before hurling it into the trash.

Then she stomped out, left Tera alone with her dad. Two against one.

Her dad rocked back in his chair. Another wink at Tera. To him, this was funny. To him, her mom was someone to make fun of. But Tera wanted to cry.

He stuck his cigarette between his lips and pointed at the trashcan. "Grab that for me, will you?"

He meant his lighter. Tera hovered over the trash, saw the lighter had sunk into the soggy ashes of her drawing. She picked the lighter out, handed it to him, her fingers stained sooty black. She wanted to wash her hands, wanted to be alone. She turned to leave, but her dad caught her arm.

"Hey." A whisper. "Did Haley really pose for that?"

"It was her idea."

"That sounds like her. But listen." He pulled on her arm until she stood in front of him, face to face. "Don't let her do that anymore. She has a big mouth, right? You don't want her blabbing to everyone."

"Okay."

"You were doing it to practice. I get that. It's not like you're a pervert. But you knew it might upset certain people, didn't you? Is that why you didn't show me?"

"I was going to," she said. "I threw the others away. This was the best one."

"You did more?" He sucked on his cigarette. "You should have shown me before you threw them away. I could have told you what

71

was good about them, what you need to work on. I could have helped you with the lighting, too." Smoke puffed from his mouth as he talked. "Where was the light coming from when you drew her?"

Tera thought for a moment. "There was a lamp," she said. "Beside the couch."

He nodded. "The shadows were all off. It looked like you were outside under the sun. Very two-dimensional."

So it wasn't good after all. Sometimes it felt like she'd never get good.

"To master the art of drawing nudes you have to capture the play of light and shadow." He drew a picture in the air with his cigarette as he talked.

"I can do better," she said.

"And how do you get better at something?"

"You practice."

"Hard to do, though, right?" He tapped ash from his cigarette. "Especially when you have a cuckoo bird for a mother?"

Tera smiled. She liked it when he called her mom a cuckoo bird. It made her seem less scary, more like a cartoon character.

"So I have an idea. I want you to keep drawing nudes." He laid his cigarette in the ashtray and put his hands on her shoulders. "But you have to be careful. We both have to be careful."

Another secret, just like the book. Another secret to gnaw at her. One time she painted that secret. A black wad in a girl's stomach. A black wad with tiny teeth. She painted it and threw it away.

"Tera," he said. "Tell me why we have to be careful."

"So the cuckoo bird doesn't find out."

"That's right." He smiled as he lit another cigarette. "So she doesn't find out and burn the house down."

CHAPTER 12

Monday after second period, I stopped at my locker to grab my Trig book. Ian was at the locker beside mine, shoving a mess of papers into his backpack. I wondered what it would feel like to be so blissfully unorganized. I'd probably be a lot more relaxed.

"Hey," Ian said.

"Hey." I pretended to be so engrossed in working my combination that I couldn't look at him. I knew he felt sorry for me. The post on the school forum had been taken down, but he probably still felt like he had to be extra nice to me.

"You doing okay?" he asked me.

"Yeah." I pulled on my lock. It didn't open.

"You need some help?"

"No, I got it." I kept my head down and spun the dial again.

"Okay, I'll see you later."

"Yeah, see you."

It took me two more tries to open my lock. I squatted down to rummage through the books at the bottom, not really looking for anything, just wanting to be invisible for a few seconds. Five more hours till the last bell, when I wouldn't have to talk to people who knew about my dad. Seven more hours till Papa Geppetto's, where no one knew anything about what had happened.

And where I'd see Joey.

A hand grabbed my elbow. I turned around, ready to spout off one of my stock responses: *It was a mistake. It's getting cleared up. Yes, I'm holding up okay.*

But when I saw who it was, my words dried up and sank like stones to the bottom of my stomach. Ellen Cornwell stood blinking at me with wide, blue-shadowed eyes. Justine Kidd hovered behind her. Both of them were Haley's friends. Justine wasn't as bad as Ellen, but Ellen was a total bitch. This was the girl who used to laugh at me for wearing the same jeans twice in one week, who called me "Paints" the first time I wore makeup to school.

"We *have* to talk," Ellen said, her face so close I could smell her Doritos breath. "Come to the bathroom."

"I can't." I slammed my locker shut. "I'll be late."

"It'll only take a minute." She tugged on my arm. "Come on."

I tried to pull away from her, but she held on. I could have tried harder, but she was the type to call after me, embarrass me even more than I already was. Sometimes it was better to get things over with. I let her herd me to the restroom.

Justine led the way and opened the door for us. Once inside, my eyes swept the open stalls. We were alone. I caught Justine looking at me in the mirror, but she glanced away when our eyes met. Then I caught my own reflection. Hunched shoulders, big eyes. A scared sheep. I straightened my spine, lifted my chin. The more fear I showed, the more Ellen would want to torment me. She was that type.

Ellen backed her butt against the sink. "I heard what happened," she told me. Who hadn't? "I wanted to make sure you're okay."

"I'm fine."

"You don't have to be brave. We're all girls here."

I laughed. "Does that make a difference?"

She looked confused for a second. Then she glared. This girl was dangerous, maybe more dangerous than Haley. "It should," she said. "Unless you're not comfortable around people in general. You seem like that type. The avoidance type."

I gritted my teeth. Haley must have put Ellen up to this. "I'm going," I said. "I don't want to be late."

"My dad's a therapist," Ellen called after me. "That's all I really wanted to say."

I stopped in my tracks, turned to face her. "Why would you think I need a therapist? My dad didn't do anything wrong."

"Oh, honey, is that what you think?" Ellen gave a wide-eyed blink. "I told Haley she was wrong, but maybe he *does* have you brainwashed."

"I'm not brainwashed," I snapped. "You have no idea what you're talking about."

"Probably true," Justine mumbled.

Ellen ignored her friend, her eyes still on me. "Haley told me what happened." Her voice dropped to a whisper. "When you were kids."

A chill prickled my scalp. What kind of lies was Haley spreading?

"She said you drew her naked. She said your dad *wanted* you to draw her that way."

Tears burned behind my eyes. "That's not true."

"Come on, Ellen." Justine tugged on her friend's arm. "Leave her alone."

Ellen let Justine pull her to the door. "If you change your mind," she called back, "call my dad's office. You want the number?"

I didn't bother answering.

• • •

The bathroom door closed behind them, shutting out the noise of the hallway. All those kids rushing to class. All those normal lives. I was about to join them, to resume trying to fit in, when my phone vibrated in my purse. I thought I recognized the number. My dad's new lawyer. I could only hope it was good news.

I flipped it open. "Hello?"

"Tera? Charlotte Gross here." She sounded breathless, in a hurry. "I set up a meeting with your father. For Wednesday."

Two days from now. I closed my eyes for a second, relief flooding over me. Dad would sign the papers, and she could start working on getting him out. "Thank you so much."

"Don't thank me yet." A rush of wind. She was probably in her car. "We have a long road ahead of us."

"I know. It's just . . ." I didn't know why I felt so grateful. I was paying her to do this. "Thanks for keeping me in the loop."

"Of course."

"So have you figured out why the police arrested him? What they have as evidence?" I knew they had the drawing, but Chase Hardy never confirmed whether or not they had a matching photo. I got rid of the print, but the digital copy might still exist. Why else would they have taken his computer?

"Like I said, I only just set up a meeting. He has to sign the fee agreement, and then I'll be on the case."

The bell rang, but I ignored it. "I wanted to ask you," I said. "Do you know what I have to do to visit him? I turn eighteen next week. Can I just show up at the jail?"

"If he wants you to visit, he puts your name on a list," she said. "They won't let you in if you're not on the list."

Dad might be so humiliated that he wouldn't want me to see him. "Can you tell him to put me on the list?" I asked. "I don't have any way to reach him."

"I'll tell him Wednesday when I see him. But you should call the jail before you visit, just to make sure."

"And you'll call me after you meet with him on Wednesday?"

"If he wants me to communicate with you, I will. Remember, I'll be working for him."

Of course he'd want her to keep me in the loop, especially after what I did for him.

I heard honking in the background. A distant siren. I wanted to keep her on the line—she was my only connection to Dad— but I couldn't think of anything else to ask.

"I have to go," she said. "I'll be in touch."

She hung up, but I kept the phone to my ear. Just for a second, so my only connection to Dad stayed with me a little longer.

• • •

The next few hours went by without anyone mentioning my dad, but I had a feeling that was about to change. I got to World History right before the bell rang so Haley wouldn't have a chance to corner me. Haley was already seated at the desk in front of mine. She watched me come in but didn't say anything.

I spent the entire class staring at the back of her head, waiting for the moment when she'd turn around and try to talk to me. But she didn't look back at all. Maybe she'd gotten in trouble for posting about me on the school forum. Maybe she was under strict orders not to talk to me.

Art was next, my last period of the day. All through high school, Art had always been my favorite class. But now I couldn't look at Mr. Stewart without feeling embarrassed by what he'd seen go on at my house.

He spent most of the class lecturing about three-point perspective, and I spent most of the class looking at my watch. Finally, the bell rang. Finally, I could go home and get ready for work. I grabbed my backpack and headed for the door.

"Tera, hang back a minute," Mr. Stewart called.

I swallowed a sigh. I could think of only two reasons why Mr. Stewart would want to talk to me after class. Either he wanted to talk about my dad or he wanted to talk about the art institute. Neither was a subject I wanted to touch. Mr. Stewart didn't care enough to help me bail out my dad, so he probably didn't care whether I went to Paris in the fall either.

Other kids jostled me as I made my way toward his desk. He waited until we were alone before speaking.

"So your mom called me last night." He took off his glasses and pinched the red marks on his nose. "She said you paid for a lawyer."

I shook my head, confused. Mom called him? Somehow I hadn't thought she was capable of such a simple thing. And why would she do that? Was she hoping he'd yell at me for being stupid? Or maybe she told him so he could talk me out of it. That didn't make sense, though. Last night she'd acted so cold, like she didn't care what I did.

"I was going to tell you," I said.

"I knew you'd get around to it."

I stared at the paperweight on his desk. The Eiffel Tower encased in glass. "I have to help my dad."

"And now you can't go to France—this year, at least."

I shrugged, like it wasn't a big deal. If I acted like I didn't care, maybe I could fool myself into believing it. Mr. Stewart was an artist, though. He studied faces. And my face was shredded.

"Okay then." He heaved a breath, blew it out. "After your mom called, I did some digging on the Internet and found this." He pulled a paper from his drawer and turned it toward me.

Attention High School Students! Win $10,000 to Put Toward Your Higher Education in Art

Hope flickered, but I tamped it down quickly. Whatever he was showing me was too good to be true. "A scholarship?" I asked.

"More like a contest. It's a cash prize for art students. The money can go toward tuition, room and board, whatever you want. I think you have a good chance of winning."

"It's not enough," I said, not willing, yet, to get my hopes up. "Ten thousand dollars isn't enough."

"No, but your mom said you're working. Maybe when all this stuff with your dad is over. Maybe then you can start saving. By the spring semester, if you win this contest . . ."

"I could have enough." His excitement started to rub off on me. My scholarship was still good for the spring semester, even without a deferral. If I won this contest, I'd only end up missing one semester.

"France is still waiting." He swept the room with his arm. "The landscapes, the culture, the amazing professors . . ."

Could it be true? Could I help my dad and still go to the art institute next spring? My eyes scanned the printout. The topic for the contest was "rain," however the artist wanted to interpret that. Any style except digital art was fair game. Contestants could upload up to three pieces to the contest website. The deadline was three weeks away.

Mr. Stewart slid the paper across his desk to me.

"Thank you." I folded it and tucked it into my purse. It felt good, knowing it was there. "You didn't have to do this."

"I wanted to." His smile was tiny and sad, but encouraging, too.

I smiled back. Maybe this would all work out. Maybe it was okay to hope.

CHAPTER 13

I shook water from my umbrella and sank into the seat behind the city bus driver. Rain pelted the tinted windows, slid down the glass in sheets. I didn't mind, though. Rain was the topic for the contest. And Mr. Stewart had once told me that rain inspired deep emotions. I looked out the window and thought about what to paint.

My mind sketched a girl on a bus, staring at her reflection in the rain-streaked window.

A man sitting in a prison yard while rain pelted his face.

The bus took a corner. I grabbed the metal pole to keep myself steady. The girl in the window held on, too, while the bus sprayed sheets of water over the sidewalk. The grating hiss of air brakes reminded me of Mom's voice.

A girl and her mother sitting on opposite ends of the couch while a storm raged outside the window.

A child standing in the rain, trying to keep her sketchbook from getting soaked.

The bus lurched. I squinted through the foggy window to see where we were. Papa Geppetto's was around the next corner. Suddenly I was nervous about my first day on the job. Would I mess up? Would I fit in? Mostly I was nervous about Joey.

A girl's face hidden in a storm cloud.

A gorgeous guy stepping into the rain to hand a girl her purse.

I pulled the cord for my stop, my stomach doing flip-flops. The rain was slowing, but I still needed my umbrella. Wet pavement, the spray of rain in my face, soaking puddles, and running footsteps. Papa Geppetto's was just across the street, but it felt like a mile. The wind caught the door when I pushed it open, blowing me inside like the swirling leaves at my feet.

Crap. And I wanted to look good for Joey.

The humid smell of yeast buried me like it always did. I made myself breathe it in, swallow it. In a few minutes I wouldn't notice it anymore.

Only one waitress was working the floor. A tall girl around my age. She slid a plate of spaghetti in front of a scrawny little boy whose parents didn't look up from their phones.

The kid stared at the plate like he wanted to throw up on it. "Meatballs are gross."

"Sorry," said the waitress. "It comes like that. I can take them off."

"I want a new plate," the kid said.

"Sure thing." She smiled without showing her teeth, rolled her eyes as soon as she turned away. Then she saw me. The smile came back. "I'll be right with you."

"That's okay," I said. "I'm looking for Mr. Barnes."

"You're the new girl?"

I nodded.

"He's in his office. You can go back there if you want."

"Thanks." I followed her behind the counter. She stopped at the big garbage pail and plucked the kid's meatballs off with her fingers. "Want one?"

"No thanks." Her nametag said *Sadie*. This was the girl who was training me. Suddenly I didn't feel nervous anymore. At least about the job.

Joey. That was another story.

My gut told me Joey couldn't possibly be interested in me, but my brain didn't want to listen. Joey knew nothing about me. For all he knew, I was a cheerleader with tons of friends. So why *couldn't* he like me? I kept replaying the few minutes I'd spent with him—how his eyes scanned my body, how his fingers lingered on my hand when he gave me back my purse, how he knew I'd be working tonight . . . He'd been flirting, definitely flirting.

I looked for him on my way to Mr. Barnes's office, trying to remember when his shift started. I thought the schedule said four o'clock. So where was he? Did he call in sick?

I heard him before I saw him. Heard him singing. Then the walk-in door swung open and there he was, right in my path. Everything inside me froze up—my heart, my gut. All the words I'd thought to say.

"Tera, right?"

I tried to move my mouth, managed to blink instead.

"I met you," he said. "You remember?"

Oh yes, I definitely remembered.

"You look lost."

"A Little Girl Lost." Wasn't that a William Blake poem where a girl meets up with a boy behind her father's back? Blake's art showed a wind-blown tree with branches like tendrils. The father's reaching fingers?

"I'm . . ." I made myself breathe. "Looking for Mr. Barnes."

"He's in his office."

"Okay, thanks." He eyeballed me as I moved past. I should have brushed my hair before I came in. I should have painted my lips with gloss.

Mr. Barnes looked up from his tiny desk when I poked my head in his office. "Hey, Tera. Good to see you."

"You, too. I forgot to ask for a uniform."

"They're in the dry storage room. You remember where that is? Go ahead and change and then I'll introduce you to Sadie."

I found my size and went to the restroom to change. Gray uniform pants, pink blouse, and a black apron. Not the most flattering outfit, but it could have been worse. At least my hair was dry, and the rain gave it some pretty waves. I stuffed my wet clothes into my backpack and glanced at my watch. Ten more minutes until my shift started. I thought about what my dad was doing right then. Did he eat in a cafeteria with other prisoners? Did they bring his food on a tray and slide it into his cell?

No sign of Joey when I came out of the bathroom. Mr. Barnes waved to me from the cash register. "Put your stuff in one of the lockers."

I took the lock and key he handed me and made my way to the back room. Joey was at the prep table, making a pizza. He didn't say anything, but again, I felt his eyes following me. Did he like what he saw? Would he still like me if I opened my mouth?

I passed him again on my way back to Mr. Barnes.

"So wait a minute," Joey said.

I stopped.

The ladle he held dripped sauce on the floor. "Is your name *Teera*, like you're crying tears? Or *Teara*, like . . ." He grinned. "Like a tear in the fabric of the universe?"

"It's *Terra*," I said. "Like the earth."

"Got it." He turned back around.

I kept walking, replaying the conversation. Should I have explained more? With the last name *Waters*, my mom thought it would be cool to name me for the land. Only she mutated the spelling so no one knew how to pronounce it. Her gift to me.

He didn't need to know all that, though. He didn't care.

Did he?

● ● ●

It all came back to me. Taking orders. Typing them into the computer. Remembering refills on drinks, remembering to bring extra napkins. I shadowed Sadie at first, but an hour into my shift I started taking my own tables. We weren't slammed, but I was busy enough that I didn't think about my dad or mom or how I might still get to go to Paris for the spring semester if I won the art contest. I didn't see much of Joey, either. His job was to make pizzas. Mine was to give everyone exactly what they wanted.

The dinner rush was over by eight o'clock. I knew I hadn't made a lot in tips, but it felt good to stir the five- and one-dollar bills I'd stuffed into my apron pocket. I finished bussing my tables while Sadie filled a plate from the salad bar. We met behind the server station.

"You hungry?" she asked. "We don't usually get a sit-down break, but Mr. Barnes doesn't mind if we grab something. You can have Joey make you a pizza."

"That's okay." The last thing I wanted was for Joey to see me stuffing my face.

"I heard my name." A shivery thrill buzzed up my spine as Joey came up behind me and grabbed a glass from the rack. "She's talking about me, isn't she?"

"You caught me," Sadie said. "I can't get you out of my head."

"Because I'm such a stud." Joey grinned at me as he filled his glass from the beer tap. He poured out the foam and took a sip. "Want some?"

I shook my head, hoping he couldn't see how flushed my cheeks were. Was he even old enough to drink?

"You sure? Mr. Barnes never notices."

"I'm not crazy about beer," I mumbled.

"I'm like you," Sadie said. "Wine is much better."

Joey took another gulp. "What is it with women and wine?"

"It's called culture, idiot. Women are cultured."

Joey snorted. "Tera might be cultured. But you, Sadie?" He refilled his glass from the tap. "You're cultured like bacteria."

Sadie rolled her eyes. "I'm surprised you know what bacteria is."

"Third-grade science. I'm smarter than I look."

"Good thing."

Joey caught me smiling. "You sure you don't want a taste? Loosen you up?"

"No thanks."

Sadie pointed her fork at Joey. "Why don't you stop guzzling so you can take Tera home. She had to take the bus here."

"Why can't *you* take her home?"

I turned away to straighten a pile of napkins.

"Liz is picking me up. We're going to Cruisers after this."

"Can I come?" Joey asked.

"You're not allowed."

"Right." Joey laughed. "So do you live close by?"

I glanced up. He was talking to me now. "Not really," I said. "It's about twenty minutes on the bus."

His eyes scanned my body, sending a trail of goose bumps up my arms. "Don't worry," he said. "I can take you home."

My insides sparked, but I kept my voice lazy. "You're sure you don't mind?"

He cocked a smile over the top of his glass. "I'll even stop drinking this amazingly crappy beer, just to keep you safe."

"Wow." I flashed him a smile, the flirty kind, I hoped. "You must really like me."

● ● ●

I wanted to paint Joey. Take this memory while it was still good and capture it forever.

Joey didn't know anything about me. With Joey, I was free to be someone else. Not the Tera with no friends. Not the Tera whose dad was in jail. And not the Tera who'd dated Alex Young.

Alex. I still cringed when I thought of him. I was a junior, and he was a senior. We had the same psych class, but I didn't even know his name until he asked me out.

He wasn't cute, not even close. But it felt good to be liked, so I found things to like about him. His long eyelashes. The way his jeans hung low on his waist. His shoes.

He took me to the two-dollar movie in Taylorville. A half-hour drive on the highway so he could save a few bucks. That was fine, I told myself. He kissed me when we got back to the car, pushing his tongue as far into my mouth as it would go. I kissed him back the best I knew how. It didn't feel good, but I kept going. His hands hurt, the way they squeezed my breasts like stress balls. But I let him do that, too, because I wanted him to like me. Then his cold fingers tried to dig under my bra. That's when I pulled away.

"What?" He sat up, breathless. "You don't like that?"

I shook my head. The windows of the car were foggy.

"Don't tell me you're a lesbian."

That hurt. I'm not sure why, but it did. The way he said it, maybe, like there might be something wrong with me. "No," I said. "It's just . . ." My voice stopped making words. I didn't have any words. How do you ask a guy to stop and still have him like you?

I was clueless. And of course, he ended up hating me. To anyone who'd listen, I was a boring lesbian who, by the way, was ugly as shit.

Haley was the one who told me all this.

"No one believes it," she said, cornering me in the restroom. "But I thought you should know."

Thanks, Haley. Always good to know.

That thing with Alex . . . That was a memory I couldn't paint. It hurt too much.

●　●　●

Before I knew it, my watch said ten o'clock and Mr. Barnes was locking the door. Mr. Barnes sat at a booth checking off the receipts for the night, while Joey, Sadie, and I tore through our side-work. My job was to roll silverware into napkins and fill the Parmesan and red-pepper shakers.

By ten-thirty, we were finishing up. I looked around for Joey. He was in the back somewhere. Hopefully he hadn't forgotten about taking me home. He seemed like the kind of guy who might forget.

Sadie plunked the mop into its bucket. Her friend was knocking on the other side of the glass door. "My ride's here," Sadie said. "Would you mind dumping the mop water for me?"

"Yeah, sure." It would give me an excuse to find Joey.

Sadie waved as she pushed open the door. Her friend took her hand and they headed off. Mr. Barnes locked the door behind them.

"You can go," Mr. Barnes told me. "Did you have a good night?"

"Pretty good."

I wheeled the mop bucket down the hallway. Joey stood at one of the stainless-steel counters pumping oil from a plastic jug into pizza pans. He looked up when I came in.

"Hey! It's the woman I gave up drinking for. You ready to go?"

I smiled as I dumped the mop water into the floor drain. "Are you ready to take me?"

"Oh yes." He winked as he squirted a shot of oil into a pan. The oil splattered onto his hands. He wiped it off on his apron.

"Messy," I said.

He grinned at me. I smiled back.

So far, so good.

● ● ●

This was it. Alone in the car with Joey. He drove a red Camaro with torn-up seats. The engine was loud. The ashy smell of stale cigarettes reminded me of Dad's studio. I tried to relax, but my body wouldn't cooperate. I felt like a bad actor—*shy girl tries to be cool.* Maybe he wouldn't notice.

"So where do you live?" Joey shifted into reverse and started backing out.

"Take El Dorado to Main and turn left. Then keep going till you hit Forest Street. I'm almost on the corner of Main and Forest."

"Got it."

His hand reached toward me. I tensed. But he was only turning up the radio. Did he really like the song, or was he tuning me out? I clutched my purse tighter. I should say something.

"Thanks for doing this."

"No problem." He grabbed his pack of cigarettes off the dashboard. "Want one?"

"No thanks." Would he like me better if I smoked? Even I knew that was stupid.

He lit up with the car lighter and took a deep drag. I liked the way he held the cigarette between his thumb and index finger. I liked how he cracked the window to blow the smoke outside. "So what are you into?" he asked.

"Um . . ." Not a hard question, but my mind froze up.

"You ever go to any of the clubs around here?"

"Huh-uh. I'm only seventeen. Well, eighteen next week. Don't you have to be twenty-one to get into those places?"

The streetlights flickered over his face as he spoke. "My uncle owns a bar in Maroa. A lot of people know him, so I don't get carded much. And if I do, I have one of these." He dug into his back pocket and handed me his wallet. "Open it."

I ripped open the Velcro fastening. In the little plastic window was a driver's license. My own license had a red background to show I was under twenty-one. His didn't have that.

"Pretty good, right?"

I handed the wallet back. "Aren't you afraid you'll get caught?"

"I can't worry about shit like that." He took another drag off his cigarette. I liked how he squinted to keep the smoke out of his eyes.

So back to his question. What did I like to do? I liked to read. Boring. And of course I liked to paint. Not that boring. A lot of people thought artists were cool. I just needed to say it the right way, so he didn't think I was weird or snotty.

He braked suddenly and turned the wheel. I grabbed the passenger door to keep from sliding into him.

"Shit, sorry about that. Almost missed the turn."

"That's okay." I peered into the darkness, getting my bearings. My street was a few blocks up. "So I'm an artist." I pulled my purse closer to my stomach. "You asked me what I like to do."

Joey turned up the volume on the radio. Too loud. "These guys are insane!" he shouted. "Have you heard of them?"

I tried to make sense of the jarring sounds. "Who is it?"

"Strapping Young Lad. The song's called 'Love.'" He turned the volume back down. "You were saying?"

"Nothing." More fiddling with my purse. The fake leather was cracking. "Just that I like to paint."

"That's cool. My mom used to draw a lot." He blew smoke out in a long stream. "That was before she went to prison."

My head shot up, my mind on high alert. Why would he tell me that?

"She's an addict." He flicked his cigarette out the window. "She tried to rob a 7-Eleven. Shot someone."

Jesus! Was he kidding?

"I just wanted to tell you that before I ask you out."

Ask me out? I turned to look at him, my heart pounding.

"So you want to go out Wednesday?" he asked. "We both have the night off."

"Sure." Inside my head, explosions were going off, but my words came out sounding calm and cool. "Wednesday's good."

"It doesn't scare you that my mom killed someone?"

Should I tell him about Dad? Would that make him feel better? The car slowed. "You said Forest Street, right?"

"Yeah." I waited for him to turn the corner. "That's my house. The green one."

He pulled into the driveway and stopped. Light shone through the curtains. Mom must be up waiting. I knew I should go before she came outside and embarrassed me.

But I didn't reach for the door handle. Not yet. The air in the car felt charged. I didn't want to mess this up.

He draped his arm over the steering wheel and turned to face me. This was it. Was he going to kiss me? We looked at each other in the dark car, him smiling a little. Me with my heart in my throat. Then he leaned in. I closed my eyes, braced myself.

His lips were soft, gentle. Nothing like Alex's. I felt my back relaxing, my lips moving in response. I pushed closer, breathed Joey in, let him soak into me. A good kisser. Definitely a good kisser.

I wanted to keep going, but he pulled away. Gently. "I've been wanting to do that all night." Again, the little smile.

"Me, too." I sounded breathless. I *was* breathless.

"God, I love this song." He reached past my arm and cranked up the volume, the bass so loud it rattled my teeth. I sat for a second, just in case, but he was busy lighting another cigarette, his head bobbing to the music.

That was my cue. I pulled the handle and got out, waved as I shut the door. He didn't see me, but that was okay. In that moment, everything was okay. I ran up to the house and looked back. Maybe he'd beep his horn, but his car was disappearing around the corner, the thump of his booming bass trailing him like a fading memory.

• • •

Mom wasn't waiting up after all, but she had left the light on for me. I stripped off my work clothes and looked at myself in the full-length mirror on the back of my bedroom door. What would Joey see if he saw me naked? Automatically, my brain started filling in the details of how I'd paint myself in the nude. I knew what areas I'd shadow, what body parts I'd turn to the light.

I had to stop myself from going down to Dad's studio to paint. I might start off trying to paint myself beautiful, but with the way I was feeling—all my emotions in turmoil because of what had happened with my dad—I wasn't sure what might come out on the canvas. A girl's shadow, sliced into ribbons by slashes of intruding light. A woman running against a threaded texture of red and black and green and yellow. The inside of a girl's head, a jungle of working gears, with bolts and screws holding things together.

And those ideas wouldn't win any contests. At the school library, I'd looked up the winners from previous years. All the paintings showed happy or touching scenes. Norman Rockwell slices of ordinary life. Nothing like what was in my head.

So instead of painting another self-portrait, I pulled out the giant stuffed lion I kept under my bed and rested my head on its body. This time I pretended the lion was Joey. I imagined I could hear his heartbeat. I imagined Joey's hand tracing the curve of my back, his arm holding me close. I imagined other things, too. And after I was done imagining, I had an idea.

I knew what to paint for the art contest.

CHAPTER 14

Wednesday promised to be a good day. Charlotte Gross was meeting my dad for the first time. I was going out with Joey that night. Haley was absent from World History. And I had a folder of sketches to show Mr. Stewart. My ideas for the art contest.

I wanted Mr. Stewart to like them as much as I did, so I was nervous when I took the manila folder up to his desk after class. He was jotting something down in his grade book.

"Mr. Stewart?"

"Tera." He eyed the folder and slipped his pen into his blazer. "You have something to show me?"

"If you have time."

"For you, I always have time. Let's move over to the window."

I clutched my folder and followed him to the window where a patch of weak sunlight fell on a long table. One by one I laid out what I'd done. A profile of a gorgeous guy, rain droplets falling from his hair. A portrait of that same guy leaning against a brick wall, his face turned up to the falling rain. A wide view of him walking in the rain, water splashing around his shoes.

Mr. Stewart straightened each sketch. I waited as he lined them up in a perfect row. He was thinking of what to say.

"Hmm," he began, but didn't add anything. He touched the corners of each drawing.

"What do you think?" I finally asked. "I have my favorite. The one with the brick wall. I like the way you can see the rain splashing on his face."

"Yes, that's probably the best of the three." Mr. Stewart scratched his nose. "And you did these recently? After we talked about the contest?"

"Yes." Why would he ask that?

"I'm sorry, Tera." He turned his head my way but didn't make eye contact. "The rain concept is there, I guess, but I'm not seeing what you want me to see."

I bit down on my lip. Hard, to keep it from shaking. "He's a guy I met. I felt inspired, just like you talk about."

"Yes, I get that. So he's some kind of bad boy?"

"What?"

"Never mind. What I meant to say was . . . When I look at these, I don't feel inspiration or love or infatuation. Whatever it is you're going for here, I'm not feeling it."

Anger swept over me. Mr. Stewart was old, in his thirties. He didn't get it. I fought to keep my voice level. "Okay."

"Can I be honest?" he asked.

I nodded. Much safer than trying to talk.

"These look more like pictures from one of those teen magazines. *Tiger Beat* maybe? I don't know all the names."

Tiger Beat? I didn't even know what that was. "He's not from a magazine," I said. "He's a real person."

"I understand that, and I get that. I'm not taking away from what you're feeling for him. I just think they're . . ." He swept his hand over the row of sketches. "Trite."

Such a smothering word, like a rag stuffed in my mouth. I tried to breathe. Got nothing.

"I'm sorry, Tera."

I stared at my sketches, tears biting behind my eyes. When I'd drawn them, I'd felt excited, hopeful. But Mr. Stewart thought they were trite.

"You can go deeper," he was saying. "These sketches don't capture your muse. They don't capture your innermost self, that part of you that's been hurt, that's suffered. You have so much pain inside and—"

"I wasn't going for pain." I shuffled the drawings into a pile. "Not everything has to be about my dad."

"I know that, Tera. That's not what I'm saying."

"You talk about good artists defying expectations. Well, that's what I'm doing and suddenly that's not what you want."

"You misunderstand. I want you to extract what's inside. That's what people want to see."

Of course they did. Haley, Ellen, everyone in the hallways who stared at me or asked me what was up with my dad . . . They all loved to see me squirm. I shoved the sketches back into the folder, not caring how the paper bent and tore. "So my life is a freak show."

"That's not what I meant."

I knew it wasn't—he was trying to help—but how do you tell someone you don't want to go digging around inside yourself because you're afraid of what will happen? If I went digging, a piece might rattle loose, and then another and another, and before I knew it, my whole self would start to crumble.

Mr. Stewart lowered his voice. "Is something else going on, Tera? Did something happen?"

Yeah, something happened. I met a guy. He made me happy. And now you're ruining it. "Nothing happened," I said.

"All right." He looked around like he was searching for what to say. "This contest. You have it in you to win it."

"These sketches were done from memory," I said. "If I had a live model, they could be a lot better."

"I don't doubt that. You can try it. But try some other things, too, okay? Play around with the rain concept. There's still time."

"I know."

"Just dig deep, okay?"

"I have to go," I said.

•••

I stumbled outside into the sunshine. Strange, after months of winter, to feel warmth soaking into my skin. My phone vibrated in my purse as I waited to cross the car lane. By now, I recognized the number.

Take a moment. Breathe.

"Hello?"

"Tera, it's Charlotte Gross. I met with your dad."

A car honked, close enough to make me jump. Haley sat in the car queue behind the wheel of her mom's Audi. She rolled her window down and waved her arm at me. A queen in her chariot.

I turned my back, pressed the phone to my ear. "Thanks for calling. Did he sign the papers?" She couldn't start helping him until he signed the papers.

"Tera!"

I tried to ignore Haley's shout, tried to concentrate on what Charlotte Gross was saying.

"He signed, but he wasn't happy about it. You should probably talk to him."

"Tera, get in! I need to talk to you!" The car behind Haley's beeped its horn. She was holding up the line. I plugged my other ear. I had no interest in sharing the details of my life so she could blab them to the whole school.

"He knows I can't visit him yet, right? Not until I turn eighteen."

"He knows."

Haley's car rolled past me. I wanted to ask Charlotte Gross something else, something important, but I couldn't think.

"I have to go," the lawyer said. "I'll be in touch."

A tick of silence. *Wait!* Haley's brake lights blinked on, then off. Traffic swelled in behind her.

"Hello?"

Too late. The line was dead.

Shit. I wanted to ask if Dad had put me on the visitors' list yet. And I wanted to ask how he looked. Was he scared? Did he seem hopeful?

Of course Haley ruined that for me.

CHAPTER 15

Joey was late. Seventeen minutes and counting.

Mom paced the living room. Like it mattered to her if he showed up. I sat on the couch, my purse clenched tight. I tried not to check my watch.

"Are you sure you have the right night?" Mom said. "Maybe he changed his mind."

A moment of panic. *Did* I have the right night? "You're not helping, Mom."

"I'm just saying what you're thinking."

"Then don't say anything. Please."

"I've dated before, Tera. Believe it or not." She bumped my leg as she paced. "How old did you say he was?"

"Around my age."

"Still in high school?"

"I think so."

"You think so?" She stopped in her tracks and turned to look at me. "How can you not know that?"

A car engine outside. Loud and getting louder. *Please let it be him!*

Headlights flashed across the picture window before turning into the driveway. I took a breath. Relief. Fear. They felt the same.

Mom pulled back the curtains and looked out. "Tell me he's not driving a motorcycle."

"Stop, Mom, he'll see you. It's just his car."

"I don't care if he sees me. Are you sure that's a car?"

"It's old."

"Where's he taking you?"

"I don't know. Please get away from the window."

"You don't know?"

The car honked. I jumped from the couch. "I have to go."

"No way." She stepped in front of me. "He's coming inside after making you wait like that."

"Mom, that's stupid."

"You're not a dog that comes when he calls."

My jaw ached. Everything about her exhausted me. If I ignored her, she'd chase me outside like a lunatic. "Fine," I said. "I'll go get him." I managed not to slam the door behind me.

Joey's red Camaro sat idling in the driveway, seeping light and smoke like some kind of alien ship. I shielded my eyes against the glare of headlights. Cold air needled my skin.

The passenger door swung open. Warmth and music flooded out. Joey leaned across the seat, his hand on the door. "You ready to go?"

"Uh." I felt like a little kid to have to say it. "My mom wants to meet you."

"Yeah, okay." No sigh. No flicker of annoyance. I tried not to stare as he glided out of the car. Jeans and a t-shirt never looked so good.

"I feel like I should warn you," I said.

"About what?"

"My mom can be a little . . ." *Tense* didn't begin to describe it, so I went for the truth. "Crazy."

He laughed. "You forget. I have one of those, too."

Something in common. We both had screwed-up moms.

Our shoes crunched on the gravel. I watched my stretched shadow, jealous of how it bobbed along without a care in the world. When we reached the door, I stopped to take a breath.

"Don't worry," Joey said. "I've done this before."

Of course he had. I turned the knob, squinting in the glut of yellow light. Mom sat on the couch with her legs tucked up, a gardening magazine in her lap. She must have snatched it from the pile next to the couch. She looked up like we'd surprised her.

"Mom," I said. "This is Joey."

"Hey," Joey said.

"I'm Connie." Then she corrected herself. "Mrs. Waters."

"Nice to meet you." Joey offered his hand. Mom shook it.

This was going too well. I had to get him out before things blew up. "So," I began. "I'll see you later, Mom."

"Just a minute." She aimed her smile at Joey, sweet, like rotten fruit. "Where are you taking her?"

Oh crap. Here it came.

"I thought we'd go to a movie," Joey said.

"Really?" Mom looked down at her magazine, still smiling that overripe smile. "Which movie?"

Joey hesitated, glanced at me.

My mind whirled, got nothing. "We're still deciding."

"I see." Her smile dissolved. The magazine slapped shut as she speared Joey with her stare. "And did you plan on feeding her first?"

Jesus, Mom!

Joey tried to laugh. "Yeah, of course. My uncle owns a restaurant."

"And which restaurant is that?"

"It's called Johnny's."

"Sounds like a male strip club."

This was getting bad. "Mom, we have to go."

She coiled her magazine into a cylinder, gripped it like a stick. "Maybe you wouldn't be in such a hurry if your boyfriend could get here on time."

"Uh." Joey rubbed the back of his neck. "I had car trouble."

"Mom, we're going." I grabbed the doorknob, shoulders hunched as if to make myself a smaller target for Mom's abuse. Joey was right behind me.

"Enjoy your night," Joey said, and I caught a glimpse of her face as I closed the door. Scared. She looked scared.

Don't think about her. Don't let her ruin this.

Cool night air washed over us. I filled my chest with it.

Joey laughed. "What the fuck?"

"Sorry," I said. "I'm so sorry."

"It's not your fault."

He led me to his car, opened my door. I climbed inside, my body rigid in the empty silence. When he slid in beside me, his smell filled the car. Soap and tobacco, his hair wet from a shower.

He dug his keys from the pocket of his jeans. "You look great."

"Thanks." I studied my hands, made sure they weren't shaking. He thought I looked great. Was that something guys said out of habit? He couldn't know how I'd tried on all the clothes in my closet before settling on my one pair of A&F jeans and a purple sweater.

"So you want to go to my uncle's place?" He started the car and twisted in his seat to face me. "It's kind of a drive."

"Maroa, right?"

"Did I mention that?"

"I forgot to tell you. I have ESP."

"Awesome." His fingers traced paths over my temples. I wanted to draw those fingers, stick them in my mouth and taste them. "So what am I thinking now?" he asked.

I closed my eyes, trying to dial the right words. Something clever, flirting. Anything but silence.

"Come on, girl." His voice teasing.

"Um." I opened my eyes. Sometimes the words came easy. Most of the time they didn't. "You're thinking you're hungry?" I asked.

"Hmm." He cocked a smile, his voice like a rumble. "Close enough."

● ● ●

We sped toward Maroa, his stereo blasting. He told me about all the different bands on his mix CD: Sleigh Bells, Cage the Elephant, Death Cab for Cutie. The music made things easier. No awkward silence, no struggling for the right words. I leaned my head against the seat and watched how his head weaved to the music, how his lips murmured the words.

The soaring beat of Jack White's "Love Is Blindness" hit me hard. The rawness of the guy's voice. The melody. Joey must have felt it, too. His hands gripped the steering wheel. His head swayed with the chords. Near the end of the song, he reached across the seat and grabbed my hand. Intense. I felt the beauty of the song. The pain.

And he shared it with me.

As the last chords faded, Joey loosened his grip. "I love the orgasm of that song."

I smiled. "Since when do songs have orgasms?"

"Since always. You never noticed? The orgasm is the part where everything explodes. The part you have to crank up."

The part where Joey had grabbed my hand. Once he took it away, my hand felt cold. "I get it," I said. "I think that's my new favorite song."

"Awesome." His tone was edged with pride. "So what *used* to be your favorite song?"

"I don't know." Did I have one? "Maybe the U2 version?"

A slow smile. "Most people wouldn't know that."

I didn't tell him how I grew up listening to U2 because my mom had all their songs. There were a lot of things he didn't know about me. Like how important art was to me. I needed to tell him about the contest. I needed to ask him to sit for me as my live model so I could paint him. But now didn't seem like the right time. I'd only come off sounding awkward.

He popped the CD out of the player, handed it to me. "Here. Take it home."

"Really?"

"I'll burn another one."

I slipped the disc into my purse, hoping I wouldn't scratch it. Should I ask if he had a case? Better not push my luck.

"So do you play something?" I asked. "An instrument?"

"Bass." Again, that tinge of pride. "I'm in a band."

"I knew it! I *do* have ESP."

"I guess you do." He rummaged through a pile of CDs on his dashboard and fed one into the player. "This is my band. We're called The Wake."

A mesh of guitar and drums pumped from the speakers. Screaming vocals. I tried to pick out the bass line but couldn't find it.

"Only problem is . . ." He turned the volume down. "We lost our drummer. It's hard to get gigs without a drummer."

"What happened?"

"Rehab. They won't let him out."

"Was he in an accident? I mean . . ." I realized too late he was talking about drug rehab.

Joey gave me a sidewise glance. "He OD'd. That means overdosed. I keep forgetting how innocent you are."

And then his hand reached over and stroked my thigh, a warm caress that jolted my insides, made me gasp. He looked over with a little smile.

I didn't need ESP to know what he was thinking: *Innocent, yes, but not for long.*

Or maybe that's what *I* was thinking.

• • •

Maroa, population 1,601. We passed two churches, a trailer park, and a grain elevator. Just behind the convenience store sat a low-roofed building made of white concrete bricks. *Johnny's* in big black letters was painted on the side.

Joey led me across the gravel parking lot. A woman came out the door, tottering on her high heels, trying to balance her cigarette and wine glass while she talked on her phone. I felt her eyes on me as we went inside.

Joey said it was a restaurant, but it looked more like a bar—the room dark, the few scattered tables made for standing around, not eating. Eighties music pumped from a jukebox. My parents' favorite.

Joey put his mouth close to my ear so I could hear him. "Let's say hi to my uncle."

I followed him to the bar. I could have sworn the guys were checking me out, and by *guys* I meant men my dad's age. No one seemed to be younger than forty. Joey hooked a stool, and I sat at the bar. He put his hand on my back. Then he draped himself over the bar like a lazy cat and waved his arm at the bartender. "Hey! Uncle Johnny!"

Joey's uncle was big—muscular big, like a wrestler. A tattoo of a snake curled up his neck and over his shaved scalp. He plunked a drink in front of a laughing woman across the bar, then grabbed an empty mug and started filling it from the beer tap. He nodded at Joey. "About time you showed up. Your dad's been looking for you."

I felt invisible while they continued their conversation.

"I told him I was going out," Joey said.

"Well, he don't remember much of what you tell him." His uncle set the full mug in front of Joey before flicking his eyes to me. "Who's this?"

Should I introduce myself? I sat on my hands and pretended to study the colorful bottles behind the bar.

"She works at Papa Geppetto's," Joey said. "She's new."

"And you let him take you out?"

It took me a second to realize he was talking to me now. I tried to come up with a witty response, but all I could do was shrug.

"Can you get her a drink?" Joey asked.

"What do you like?"

I opened my mouth to order a pop, but Joey beat me to it.

"She'll have wine. You like wine, right?"

"Uh, sure."

His uncle plucked a wine glass from the rack above his head. "White, pink, or red?" he asked me.

"Pink's fine."

"Pink it is." He opened a fridge beneath the bar and pulled out a bottle. The wine glass was small, but he poured it full and set it down in front of me. No ID required.

"Thanks." I lifted the glass to my mouth. Both of them watched me like I was performing some kind of dare. The first sip went down smooth.

"You like it?" Joey asked.

"It's good." I took another sip.

"You hungry? You want fish and chips?"

"That's fine."

"Get her the special," he told his uncle. "And I'll have another beer."

While his uncle got the beer, Joey leaned in close so he could talk in my ear. "If my dad shows up and starts bothering you, just ignore him."

I nodded like it wasn't weird at all that his dad might show up and bother me.

His uncle set a full mug in front of Joey and another glass of wine in front of me, even though I'd only drunk half of what I had. "So you don't fall behind," he said.

Was he joking? I smiled and took another sip.

Joey looked around the bar. "So where is he?" he asked his uncle.

"Downstairs."

"Loaded?"

"Sleeping it off."

I felt like I was eavesdropping on a private conversation, like I wasn't needed there at all.

"Any chance we'll see him in the next hour?" Joey asked.

"He's about due to come wandering around." His uncle squirted something from a hose into a fancy glass and stuck a straw into it. Then he added a shot of brown liquor. He set the glass in front of a man across the bar. The man looked up and met my eyes. He winked. I looked at my glass.

My glass was empty, the first one at least. I pushed the empty glass to the side and started in on the second. A new song started playing. Kajagoogoo's "Too Shy." Joey kept looking around the bar, and I kept looking at Joey, waiting for him to make conversation. At least the wine was helping. Slowly, some of the tension evaporated from my shoulders. Joey's uncle smiled at me and poured me another glass.

I was halfway through my second drink when my food arrived. By then, I felt amazing. Relaxed like I'd never been. Smiling. Uncle Johnny set the platter of fish and chips in front of me, but I was having too much fun to eat. My whole body swayed to the music. Joey eyed me with a little smile. Wow.

He said something, but I couldn't hear him over the music. I shook my head, slow and luxurious, like I was moving underwater. He leaned in to yell in my ear. "You look pretty sexy!"

Even my smile felt relaxed. Was this real? Then he kissed my neck, and a flush like a warm bath shivered up my body.

His breath warmed my neck. I pushed closer, felt my stool start to topple. Joey's hand on my arm kept me from falling.

"Careful," he said.

I laughed, not embarrassed at all.

He pointed at my plate of fish. "Your food's getting cold."

"I guess I'm not hungry."

Another glass of wine appeared in front of me.

"Hey, look," Joey tapped my arm. "My dad."

I followed his eyes to where a tall skinny guy with a beard was clutching the backs of chairs as he shuffled toward the bar. His chestnut hair was the same color as Joey's, but messy, like he'd just woken up. His messy hair reminded me of my dad's mug shot. I tried to swallow my uneasiness.

"Dad!" Joey waved him over.

I put down my drink as he stumbled his way over. Now I knew how Joey had felt when I'd made him meet my mom.

"Don't worry," Joey said in my ear. "He won't remember anything."

Up close, I saw how much Joey looked like him. Besides the chestnut hair, they had the same hazel eyes, the same lips. But his dad's face was puffy and sweaty, his eyes glassy. His mouth hung open. I'd seen old guys stare at me like that before. Greedy.

"Dad, this is Tera," Joey said.

His eyes shot from my chest to my face. "What'd you say?"

"I'm Tera," I yelled.

"Oh." His smile was missing teeth. "I'm Tom. Call me Tommy." He stuck out his hand, and I shook it. His sweaty hand swallowed mine.

"You finished eating?" Joey asked me.

I nodded. Joey's dad kept staring.

"Want to go downstairs?" Joey asked.

"Uh." I wasn't sure what was downstairs, but it had to be better than getting ogled by a guy who looked like he'd crawled out of the gutter. "Sure."

As soon as I stood up, my head started spinning. When I tried to walk, my legs wobbled. Joey seemed to know I was having trouble. He didn't let go of my hand as we weaved between tables toward a little alcove at the other side of the bar. A cigarette machine stood between two doors labeled *Dudes* and *Chicks*. Across from the restrooms was a third door that said *Employees Only.* Joey pulled it open. A narrow staircase led down.

"Go ahead." Joey held the door for me.

I felt my way down like a blind person. "I think I'm drunk," I announced, and Joey laughed. Then I almost rammed my face into a closed door at the bottom of the stairs.

Joey reached around me and pushed open the door. Dark inside. Music from the bar vibrated the walls. It smelled like a basement. It *was* a basement. He groped the wall for a light switch, and suddenly I could see. Boxes were stacked ceiling-high on metal utility shelves that ran the length of the room. Shoved against the far wall was a futon, and on the arm of the futon was an ashtray overflowing with cigarette butts. A mini-fridge squatted beside the futon. Was his dad sleeping down here? Did he *live* here?

"What is this place?" My voice sounded way too loud.

"My dad's flophouse." Joey rubbed the back of his neck. It was the first time I'd seen him look embarrassed. "Sorry," he said. "We can leave. I didn't realize how this must look."

"That's okay." This was awful, but it wasn't Joey's fault. "So you don't live with your dad?"

"Not really."

What did that mean? Was Joey homeless?

"It's temporary," Joey explained. "Until we can find a place."

He *was* homeless. Oh my God. I longed for the right words, something to let him know I didn't judge him.

"My dad's in jail," I blurted.

That surprised him. He blinked at me like maybe he hadn't heard me right.

"He hasn't been convicted or anything, but . . ." My voice trailed off. I waited for him to ask what my dad had done—what he had been accused of doing.

"No shit." A slow grin spread across his face. "I knew there was something about you."

"I was going to tell you earlier, but . . ." I shrugged.

"Don't let it bother you. My dad's a total fuckup, but it's *him* fucking up, not me."

He was right. I didn't have to feel embarrassed by my dad. But I still did.

Joey moved the ashtray from the arm of the futon onto the floor. "Sorry I don't have a better place to take you. You want to go back?"

Back home? Back upstairs? All I wanted was to be with him. He made me feel pretty. He made me feel special. "No," I said. "I'm fine."

"You want to sit?" He gestured to the futon. "At least we can talk."

"Talking is good."

He led me to the futon and we sat, our legs touching. He reached over, traced the outline of my lips. A sudden flush warmed my body, made me brave enough to meet his gaze. I stared at him, marveling at how absolutely gorgeous he was. His face so perfectly proportioned. Hazel eyes, straight eyebrows, and long, dark lashes.

"I drew you," I blurted.

"That's cool. How'd it turn out?"

"Good," I said. *Trite.*

"Can I see it sometime?"

"Sure." So did that mean he wanted to see me again? "Actually," I said. "I was wondering if you'd model for me."

"You mean for a photo shoot or something?"

"For a portrait. So I can paint you."

"Seriously?"

"It's for a contest. First prize is ten thousand dollars, and I need to win it so I can go to art school in Paris. I already have a scholarship, but I need money for an apartment and food and a plane ticket and all that."

He raised his eyebrows. "You're really that good?"

"They already accepted me."

"I mean, are you really good enough to win ten thousand dollars?"

"I don't know. Maybe. I think so. But I need to paint something really amazing. It has to have something to do with rain. And the deadline's less than two weeks away."

"And you want to paint me."

"I'd have to get your hair wet. Your clothes, too."

He laughed.

"Don't laugh. I think it'll mean something." It *would* mean something.

"I just think you're funny. But in a good way."

"So you'll let me paint you? You'll sit for me?"

He took a swig of his beer. "Yeah, sure."

"Can you come over to my house in the next couple days?"

"I have to come over?"

"Well, yeah." I looked at my hands. "That's where all my stuff is to paint. I guess I could bring it to your place, but . . ." He didn't have a "place." He and his dad were living in the basement of a bar.

Joey slouched on the futon and leaned his head back. "Sure, I'll come over."

"Really?"

"Is this going to make me famous?"

"Famous?" I laughed. "It might be published somewhere, but I have to win first."

"And you think you can win."

"My art teacher thinks so, too. Can you come over Friday afternoon?" I had school and work on Thursday. Friday would be the soonest I could do it. "Around four?" I said. "Because I really need to get started on this."

"Yeah, sure. Friday. Whatever you want." He set his beer bottle on the floor. "But right now, I want to give you a massage."

"Okay," I said. I wanted to make sure he knew how important coming over was, but I didn't want to nag him about it.

"Close your eyes," he said. "Lean your head back."

I did what he asked. As soon as he touched me, all thoughts of the contest went out of my head.

I trembled as his hand trailed down my spine. He moved closer, his warm lips on my neck, his fingers tracing the V-neck of my sweater. His hand moved lower, between my breasts and down my stomach.

"You like that?" he murmured in my ear.

I couldn't talk. I could only shudder.

He moved up beside me, slowly turned my face toward his. And then his lips were on mine. He pressed into me, and I leaned back on the futon, let him lower himself on top of me. His lips on my mouth, my throat, his hands sliding down my chest, clutching my breasts like he couldn't get enough. I wrapped my legs around his hips and pushed against him. He moaned in his throat, and all I wanted was to hear that sound—proof that he wanted me like I wanted him.

So when his hands pulled off my sweater, I didn't stop him. And when he fumbled with my bra, I helped him with the clasp. The lacy red straps lay loose on my shoulders. He grabbed the bra in his fist and tossed it.

And there I lay. The goods. Exposed and shivering.

He leaned back on his heels and watched me with hooded eyes, his mouth slack, his face flushed and sweaty.

Like his dad. He looks like his dad.

Cold, I crossed my arms over my chest.

"It's okay," he said.

And it *was* okay. I let him nudge my arms to the side while my mind struggled to remember: This was *Joey*, the guy I lay in bed and dreamed about. But in my dreams, he didn't have that look. Greedy. Like a pig. And in my dreams, he didn't make that sound. Panting. Like a dog.

I forced my eyes closed, clamped my mouth shut. *Don't say it! Don't ruin this!*

But out it slipped, the word I didn't want to say.

"Stop."

And then another, this one even worse.

"Please."

And before I knew it, I was sitting up and crying.

CHAPTER 16

Tin Man

Tera covered herself with the blanket and waited for her dad's knock. She tried to imagine she was waiting for the doctor like she'd done a few months ago for her fourth-grade physical. This was no different—better even, because this time she had a comfy blanket to huddle behind instead of a scratchy paper sheet.

The knock came. Her dad poked his head into the room. "You ready?"

"I think so."

He stepped in. The door clicked shut. "You have to take the blanket off." The camera hung from a strap around his neck.

Suddenly this was a lot scarier than being at the doctor. She pressed her arms to her sides like she was plunging down the waterslide at the public pool. Maybe her dad would see how scared she was and wouldn't make her do it. Or maybe he'd push her like Haley had pushed her down the slide so the other kids could have their turn.

"Come on, Tera." He sat at the foot of her bed. "You said you were ready for this."

"I know."

"And now you're scared?"

She nodded.

"You think Rembrandt was scared when he did it? You think van Gogh was? You say you want to be a great artist, but you're scared to follow in their footsteps."

He was mad, she could tell. But moving the blanket . . . She couldn't make herself do it.

"I know you're scared. I was scared, too, the first time I drew myself nude. Only in my day we didn't have digital cameras." He held the

111

camera up so she'd see how lucky she was.

"Artists today have it easy," he said. "You take a few pictures in the privacy of your own home, and voilà! *Instant reference material. How do you think artists who don't have nude models learn to draw the human form?"*

He waited, but she didn't have an answer. Her mom said she was smart, but sometimes she had straw for brains. Just like the Scarecrow.

"You have to see yourself in the nude," he said. "And to do that, you need photos to study."

"Can't I take the picture myself?" Maybe it wasn't the camera that scared her, but him behind the camera.

"Go ahead." He sounded friendly, but the way he whipped the camera from around his neck, she knew he was mad. It weighed more than she expected, with all kinds of buttons and dials. She almost dropped it when the blanket slipped. Her hand scrambled to cover herself.

"Not so easy, is it?" He grabbed the camera and looped the strap around his neck. "I thought you were ready for this, but maybe I was wrong. Maybe you're not a real artist."

"I am."

"Prove it, then. Three easy steps. Step one: Let go of the blanket."

She'd already done step one by accident, so doing it again should've been easy. Still, she had to concentrate to make her fingers let go. She focused on the flowered wallpaper, let the blanket slip to her waist. She tried not to notice how her bare chest moved up and down with every breath.

"Okay," he said. "Now take off the blanket. All the way."

Was this step two? She kept her eyes on the wallpaper as she peeled the blanket down her legs. When it reached her toes, she scooted into the corner of her bed, her legs out stiff.

He squinted at her. "You look like a mannequin. Give me something more natural."

"What do you mean?"

"Remember those nude figures in that book? They weren't sitting

there like naked Barbie dolls. Stretch yourself out. Imagine you're a cat."

"I never had a cat."

He rolled his eyes. "A dog, then. Imagine you're a dog."

He was losing patience. Still, she couldn't move.

"You don't know what a dog looks like? Are you really that stupid?"

"Is this step three?"

"What?"

Should she remind him about the steps? Not now. He was getting fed up.

She bent her wrists to her chest like she was begging for a doggie treat.

Disgust scrunched his face. "Jesus Christ, Tera." He pushed himself up from the bed. "If you won't do this right, I might as well leave."

"Don't leave." She hugged herself, fingers digging into her neck. "I don't know what you want me to do."

"I want you to stop acting like a scared little baby! I want you to get on your hands and knees like a goddamn dog!"

She didn't move, couldn't move. What was wrong with her that she couldn't move?

He shook his head like he didn't want to be around her anymore. "I thought you were a real artist. I thought you were my protégé."

"I am."

"Show me then."

This was her last chance. If she didn't show him, he'd get up and leave. Maybe forever.

Her body stiff like the Tin Man, she crouched before him on her hands and knees, her heart pounding in her chest. Not the Tin Man, then. The Tin Man didn't have a heart. More like the Cowardly Lion.

She snuck a look at his face. Was this what he wanted? He had that look like he was staring at a great work of art.

He pointed the camera. The lens zoomed in. She imagined drawing herself this way and thought she might cry. But she didn't. Tears would rust. At the last second, she turned her head toward the wall.

At least then she wouldn't have to draw her face.

CHAPTER 17

My tears came like a flash flood, sudden and fierce and draining. I couldn't remember the last time I'd cried. But there I was, in the basement of his uncle's bar, bawling like someone had died. What was wrong with me?

Joey reeled back, his hands in the air like he'd been caught stealing. And as suddenly as my tears had come, they stopped. I sat there on the futon with my arms crossed over my naked chest, staring at the cement floor. "I'm sorry," I mumbled. "I don't know why I'm crying."

Joey looked around like he was searching for an escape route, his eyes landing on my bright red bra. "Here." He snatched it up and tossed it into my lap. "I'll take you home."

"You don't have to."

"Then what? You want me to call a cab?"

I shook my head.

"Then what's with you?" He sat on the futon a good two feet away and rubbed his forehead like I was giving him a headache. "I like you, Tera, but I can't handle this mental shit."

He liked me—he'd said it himself. And here I was screwing it up. What could I do to make him stay? Should I scoot next to him? Pick up his hand and put it on my breast? But I couldn't bring myself to do anything except sit there with my head down. Afraid to look at him.

Joey watched me while he rubbed his eyes. I could see his patience wearing thin.

"It's just . . ." My fingers dug into my arms. "I've never done this before."

"Yeah, I kind of got that."

"And it's stupid, I know, but . . ." I stared at the bra in my lap. Why did I pick red, of all colors? Red was for confident girls.

"But what?"

Good question. My mind whirled as I turned to slip my arms into the bra straps. Why would I suddenly burst into tears when I wanted him so badly? Then it came to me—what I could say. Something that might make sense to him.

"I promised myself I'd wait," I said. "Until I turn eighteen. My birthday's so close. Next Sunday. So to get this close and screw it up . . ."

As I blurted all this out, I almost believed it. When I turned eighteen, I'd be a grownup—at least technically—and maybe that would make a difference.

Silence. I fumbled with my bra clasp. Maybe he'd reach out and help me.

"You could have just said that."

"I know." I finally got my bra fastened and turned to face him. My sweater was in his hands. He held it out to me.

Another long silence as I pulled it over my head. All the sweaters I'd tried on, and I'd chosen this one because it hugged my chest. Stupid.

"You ready?" he asked.

To go home, he meant. My sweater was on, so I guess I was. I stood.

At least he didn't seem mad anymore. I stole a look at his face. Eyes narrowed, mouth a straight line. Did he still like me? Even a little?

My legs wobbled as I followed him up the dark stairwell, and not because I was drunk. When we surfaced into the bar, I kept my eyes on Joey's back, afraid to wave goodbye to his uncle, afraid to catch a glimpse of his dad. Surely everyone in the bar was staring.

Outside, I lowered my head against the cold as I followed him to the car. If only I could rewind the night. We could be resting on the futon, my head on his chest. He could be stroking my hair. We could be laughing.

The song on his stereo picked up where it left off when I was still happy. He turned the sound down with an impatient flick of his fingers. I was about to apologize again, anything to break the awkward silence. But then he twisted in his seat to look at me, his eyebrows raised.

"So you want to try this again?"

My heart jumped. Did he want to go back inside? Have sex in the car? Did it matter? I knew my answer should be "yes" before he changed his mind.

"What I meant was . . ." He shook a cigarette from his pack and lit it. "We could go out for your birthday. Unless you have other plans."

I struggled to sound casual so I didn't look too eager. "Nothing definite," I said.

Which was a joke. With Dad in jail, I had *no* plans for my birthday. Mom's birthday duty started and ended with making a cake, and I'd be lucky if she remembered even that. Dad was the one who tried to make things special. When I was little, he took me to Chuck E. Cheese's. And when I got older, we'd get pizza delivered and eat it in front of the television with Mom's cake waiting for us on the coffee table. Up until a few years ago, I had this ritual where I'd paint a watercolor of the day so I'd always remember it. I kept the paintings in a special scrapbook decorated with ribbon to make it look like a present. Sometimes I took it out and looked at it.

Joey tapped his fingers on the steering wheel. "So your birthday's on Sunday, right? I'm trying to remember if I work that day."

I knew for a fact he didn't, but I wasn't about to tell him I'd memorized his schedule. I held my breath, watching him rub the stubble on his chin.

"I'll switch with Cam if I have to," he said. "Are you up for that? For going out on your birthday?"

"Yeah," I said. "Sure."

"We'll go somewhere nice for dinner. Somewhere special."

Tears welled up, but I froze them in place. I didn't realize, until that moment, how afraid I'd been to spend my birthday alone.

• • •

Mom was sitting on the couch when I got home. Not watching TV, not reading, just sitting there. Her pills sat on the coffee table next to a glass of water.

She blinked when I came in, like I'd woken her from a trance.

"Hey," I said.

"You're home early. What happened?"

"Nothing."

"It didn't go well?"

"It went fine. We're—" She cut me off before I could tell her how I'd be going out with Joey on my birthday.

"Something came in the mail for you." She slid a white envelope the size of a magazine off the coffee table and handed it to me.

At first, I thought it was from Dad. But if Dad had sent me anything, she would have thrown it away. When I turned the envelope over, I saw where it came from. The Paris Art Institute. I thought maybe they'd answered my request for a scholarship deferral, but their website said they'd reply by e-mail.

"I thought you might want to see it," Mom said. "Even though you're not going."

I glanced at her face. She didn't look smug, like I expected. She looked hopeful. Maybe she thought seeing mail from the art institute would make me change my mind about paying for my dad's lawyer. Didn't she know it was too late for that?

"Thanks." I made sure to keep my face neutral. I didn't want her to see how it hurt me not to be going this fall.

"Aren't you going to open it?"

"I'll open it later." I stood up from the couch, still holding the envelope. "Good night."

As soon as I shut my door, I tore the envelope open. Inside was a letter from the school, along with a course catalog. I read the letter first. The dean welcomed me to the most prestigious art school in the world and invited me to choose my classes for the coming fall semester.

I let the letter drop to my bed and turned on the laptop I'd borrowed from school. Almost a week had gone by since I'd written the school to ask for a deferral. If they were sending me a course catalog, did that mean they hadn't gotten my letter?

I did an e-mail search to see when, exactly, I'd sent my request. That's when I found their reply in my Spam folder. *Please,* I thought as I clicked it open. *Please be good news.*

> *Dear Ms. Waters,*
>
> *We received your request for deferral of your scholarship. The Institute will, if necessary, defer some scholarships for a single period of up to two years. However, your circumstances do not meet our deferment policy. If you choose not to employ your awarded scholarship for the upcoming fall and spring semesters, you will need to reapply for both admission and scholarship . . .*

I couldn't breathe. I couldn't think. I read the letter again to make sure I understood what they were telling me. I had to use my scholarship this year or I'd lose it.

The course catalog lying on my bed mocked me. *Don't look at it,* I told myself. *You can't go, so don't torture yourself.* But I picked it up anyway. On the slick front cover was a photo of the campus. The school's iconic bell tower overlooked a busy Paris neighborhood, the kind where people drink coffee at sidewalk cafés and walk to the local bakery to buy their bread. I turned to the first page and stared at the collage of photos: students painting, sculpting, sitting on hilltops with easels and paintbrushes. Teachers looking over students' shoulders at their work. Everyone smiling.

Their smiles cut through me.

I scanned the courses—all those classes I wouldn't be taking: Introduction to Sculpture. Renaissance in the Modern Age. Depth and Light for Acrylics.

I hurled the catalog across the room and it smacked against the wall. I wanted to hear a crack, a break, but all I got was a fluttering of pages. I grabbed the catalog and shoved it into a drawer.

I wouldn't be going because of Dad. It didn't matter that it wasn't his fault. A part of me still blamed him. I reminded myself that it was *my* drawing that had landed him in jail. And the photo he had taken of me naked—the one the police *might* have found on his computer? That was a mistake, the kind people make when they don't know any better. Dad was so much the artist that he was blind to the bigger picture. He'd realized, though, that it was a mistake. I'd made him realize it.

And it all seemed like a hundred years ago.

CHAPTER 18

I didn't want to paint in Dad's studio. That would have felt too much like a betrayal, as if life went on just fine while he was in jail. So Friday after school I dragged all my painting gear upstairs to the kitchen.

Then I sat in the living room to wait for Joey. Already, he was late, but I'd expected that. Mom came out of her bedroom wearing jeans and a button-up shirt. Her hair was combed. She looked nice. I'd already told her Joey was coming over. She'd promised to keep out of the way so I could paint him for the contest.

"Don't worry." She flopped onto the couch with the want ads and put her feet up on the coffee table. "I'll leave when he gets here."

"He's late," I said.

"Are you surprised?"

"Not really. I think it's a guy thing."

"Or a Joey thing."

"Mom, don't."

She opened her mouth to say something but then clamped her lips closed.

We waited. The clock on the cable box said *4:23*.

"So you really think he'll make a good subject?" she asked. "For the contest, I mean."

I fiddled with a loose thread on the chair. "Mr. Stewart said it was best if I painted him as a live model instead of from memory. So that's what I'm doing."

She squinted at the clock. "Wasn't he supposed to be here at four? Maybe you should call him."

Then my cell phone rang. It was too late in the day for Dad's lawyer to call, so I knew before looking at the number that it had to be Joey. He was probably on his way, calling to tell me he was running late.

I flipped open my phone. "Hello?"

"Hey, Tera, it's Joey."

"Hey."

Mom sat forward on the couch, mouthed some words I couldn't understand. I waved her away.

"So I can't make it over there," he said. "Something came up."

"Oh."

"Sorry," he said.

"That's okay." Had I just said that? It wasn't okay, not at all. "What happened?" I asked.

"I got busy. Helping a friend."

"Oh, okay."

"So I can't really talk. I'll see you Sunday, though. For your birthday."

"Okay. Eight o'clock, right?"

"Right. I'll see you then." He didn't wait for me to say goodbye before hanging up.

I felt Mom's eyes on me as I closed my phone and tried to act like nothing was wrong.

"He's not coming, is he?"

I shook my head. "He had to help a friend."

"A better friend than you, obviously."

"Thanks, Mom. That helps."

She got up from the couch and stretched. "I'm just saying."

• • •

Obviously I couldn't rely on Joey to sit for me, so now I had to think of something else for the contest. But what? Something to do with rain. I pressed my palms against my face. *Think!*

Mr. Stewart wanted me to paint something from my innermost self, something that showed my pain. Maybe he was right, but what did that have to do with rain?

And then I had an idea. I could paint my greatest fear. My dad living in prison. My dad in a prison jumpsuit, getting the crap beat out of him. While rain poured down from a black sky.

I looked on the Internet for pictures of prison yards. Seeing the real thing would have been better, but I had to make do.

I painted all evening and well into the night. Concrete walls and chain-link fences. Barbed wire, brick, and spurts of green grass. A single tree blooming with pale pink flowers. An overcast sky, a gauzy film of rain covering the entire scene.

But when it came time to paint my dad, I didn't know what to do, where to start. Maybe I was just tired, but I couldn't bring myself to show him with blood on his face. I didn't want to paint him in pain.

So I left it the way it was. An empty prison yard, the only movement the slant of the falling rain.

I rinsed my paintbrushes in the sink and stepped back to look at what I'd done. Not good enough. I knew it wasn't good enough. But I had time before the deadline. I could do something else.

CHAPTER 19

Sunday. My eighteenth birthday.

The first thing I did after rolling out of bed was call the jail.

"I want to schedule a visit," I told the man on the phone.

"Your name?"

"Tera Waters."

"And the inmate's name?"

"Tim Waters. Timothy."

I heard him typing. "I don't have you down here as an approved visitor."

"Are you sure?" *It shouldn't be this hard to see my dad*, I thought. "I just turned eighteen today. Maybe the computer isn't letting you see my name?"

"It shouldn't matter. How do you spell your last name?"

I spelled it out for him, heard more computer keys clacking.

"You sure you're calling the right jail? This is the Samuel L. Mast facility. Maybe he got transferred somewhere else."

"No, I have the right jail. I'll just . . ." I bit back my frustration. "I don't know. Thank you."

I hung up and tried to think. Today was Sunday. Charlotte Gross wouldn't be working. I called her anyway, got her voice mail.

"Uh, hi. It's Tera Waters. I turned eighteen today, so I just called the jail to make sure it was okay for me to visit my dad, and they said I wasn't even in their system, so I was wondering how that could be and what I should do. Did Dad not put me on the visitors' list? Call me when you get a chance. Thanks."

I closed my phone and looked at the clock on my nightstand. I'd been planning to paint before I had to go to work, but now I was too worried. Why wasn't I on the list? Did Dad not want to see me? Did he blame me for everything that had happened?

• • •

I got off work at six, which left me enough time to shower and get ready for my birthday date with Joey. As I rode the bus home, I realized I hadn't told Mom that I wouldn't be home tonight. She'd been gone all day yesterday, filling out job applications, and by the time I'd gotten off work, she was asleep. She was still asleep this morning when I left for Papa Geppetto's, so I would have to tell her about my date as soon as I got home.

It was already dark by the time the bus dropped me off near the house. Charlotte Gross hadn't returned my call, so I had no idea what was going on with the jail not letting me visit. I tried to push the worry from my mind. Joey would be picking me up soon.

I came in through the kitchen, surprised to hear "New Year's Day" blasting from a CD player on the counter. My mom's favorite song.

She didn't hear me come in. She had her back to me, cracking eggs into a mixing bowl. I almost didn't recognize her. She wore dress pants and a nice blouse. Her hair was in a French braid.

I laid my purse on the counter. "Mom?"

Her shoulders jerked and she almost dropped her wooden spoon. She turned, and for a second I thought she wanted to hug me. Instead she reached behind me to turn down the CD player.

"What are you doing?" I asked.

"What's it look like I'm doing? I'm baking you a cake." Her smile looked pasted on. "Did you forget it's your birthday?"

"No." I gripped my elbows. "But I thought *you* forgot."

"Well, that's stupid."

"Mom, this is nice and everything, but I'm going out." I bit my lip, seeing the way her face fell. "With Joey."

"Oh." Her shoulders slumped.

"Sorry. I should have told you earlier."

She laid down the spoon, then changed her mind and picked it up again. Her elbow jabbed the air as she whipped the batter. A few seconds of that and she'd be worn out.

"We have an electric mixer."

"I like doing it this way."

"Do you need help?"

"Why would I need help? This is *my* job."

"Oh." I made myself smile. "So any luck with the job hunting?"

"Please don't ask me that. I'll let you know if I find something."

I turned to go, but her voice stopped me. "Why don't you stay home tonight? Birthdays should be family time."

I was shaking my head before she got the words out. "No, Mom."

The spoon banged against the sides of the bowl. "He can have dinner with us. I got a pizza. DiGiorno. We can eat on the couch and watch a movie."

"Joey's taking me to dinner. He made a reservation and everything." I had no idea whether he'd made a reservation, but it sounded good.

She stopped stirring and bit her lip.

"Maybe next time, okay?"

She nodded.

"Thanks for making me a cake. Thanks for remembering."

I left her standing by the oven, staring at the empty cake box with watery eyes. It was hard to feel sorry for her, but I did. A little.

An hour later—showered, dressed, and sprayed with Viva La Juicy—I had time to kill before Joey came, so I kept busy by cleaning up Mom's baking mess. I was careful not to splash water on my outfit, a black miniskirt and black tights. On top I wore a gray-blue sweater that Ian had once told me looked good on me.

Mom watched me from the kitchen table. The unfrosted cake sat on a plate in front of her. "You look nice," she said.

High praise coming from her. She wouldn't be saying that if she could see underneath. Not a red bra this time, but lacy black.

Mom turned the cake plate around and around, examining the crooked layers.

"It smells good," I offered.

She sighed through her nose. "I forgot the candles."

"Next year." I shut off the water and grabbed a towel from the drawer.

"When's he getting here?"

"Eight or eight-thirty."

"Can't he pick a time and stick to it?"

I held back a sigh. "Things have changed since you dated."

"I doubt that." She pinched off a piece of cake. "I know how guys operate. I married—"

Headlights cut across the kitchen. She froze, her fingers halfway to her mouth.

I grabbed my purse off the counter. "That's him."

"He's not coming in?"

"I said I'd meet him outside."

I stiffened, waiting for her tirade, but all she said was, "Can't say as I blame you."

Was that an apology? I looked at her sharply, my hand on the doorknob. She sniffled and wiped her eyes. So not an apology. More of her feeling sorry for herself.

I was halfway out the door when she called after me. "Happy birthday, Tera."

I pretended not to hear and hurried up the driveway. Joey was waiting.

●●●

Joey wore faded jeans and a gray t-shirt with *My Chemical Romance* on the front. Gorgeous as usual. His eyes traveled the length of my body as I slid into the car.

"You look great," he said.

"Thanks."

"You ever hear this?" He turned up the volume on his stereo as he backed out of the driveway.

I listened, but it was too loud to make sense of. "I don't think so," I yelled.

"Civil Twilight," he yelled back. "They're from South Africa, but they're white." He turned the volume down. Still loud, but bearable. "So you like them?"

"Yeah, they're good."

"Sadie was right then."

"She said I'd like it?"

"She said chicks dug it. Do me a favor, okay?" He steered with his knees and reached behind him to grab a handful of CDs. He piled them in my lap. "Listen to these and tell me what you think."

I sifted through them. They were all home-burned and labeled in sloppy capital letters. I didn't recognize any of the names except *My Chemical Romance*, because it was on his t-shirt.

"And I almost forgot." He reached behind him again and came back with a red rose wrapped in crinkly plastic. "Happy birthday."

I caught my breath. No one had ever given me a flower, let alone a red rose. For homecoming and prom, kids at school could buy each other carnations and have them delivered to homeroom. Some girls got dozens and carried them around all day. I never got one, but I knew what the colors meant. Everyone knew. Yellow meant friendship. Pink meant someone liked you. But red . . . Red meant someone loved you.

Not that I thought Joey loved me or anything. But I knew he liked me. He'd said it himself.

"Wow," I said. "Thank you."

"No problem." He pushed Eject on the CD player. When the disc popped out, he handed it to me, along with an empty plastic case that looked like he'd dropped it a few times. "Can you put this in your purse?"

I lay the flower in my lap so I could fit the disc into its broken case. "So where are we going?" Somewhere downtown, maybe? That's where all the nice restaurants were.

"Red Robin." He rubbed his stomach. "They have those huge-ass burgers."

So not somewhere that required a reservation. Prickles stung my eyes. I stared at the flower in my lap, wilting already. Two of the petals lay in my lap.

He glanced over. "You hungry?"

"I think so." I poked the fallen petals. Still velvety soft. Still good. I closed my eyes, waited for the sting of tears to fade. Then I opened my billfold and stuck the petals inside. Things could be good and not perfect. The world wasn't perfect.

The thought came again, the one I'd been pushing down. Did he ask me out because I'd promised him sex? Did it matter? He wanted to be with me. And he liked me. That much I knew for sure. So what if Red Robin wasn't fancy? Any restaurant where I got to sit down and order from a menu sounded good. Maybe they did something special for people's birthdays. Maybe that's why he wanted to bring the CD.

"So do they play music there?" I asked.

He squinted at the road. "I think so. Why?"

"I never heard of a restaurant playing people's personal CDs."

He laughed. "The music's not for dinner."

"Oh."

"It's for later. You know . . ." He squinted as he lit a cigarette. "For dessert."

• • •

I sat in the booth across from Joey and scanned the menu. The Parmesan-crusted snapper looked good, but it cost way more than the burgers. Girls at school talked about ordering the most expensive thing on the menu when a boy took them out, like they were entitled or something. I never understood that. The last thing I wanted was for Joey to think I was mooching off him.

He looked up from his menu and smiled at me. "Get anything you want."

I smiled back. Maybe he'd read my mind.

A gray-haired waitress came to our table and rattled off the specials like a robot. I glanced at her nametag. *Carol.* Joey pointed to a huge bacon cheeseburger on the menu. "Give me the Pig-Out Tavern Double." Beside it was a big red star with white letters. *Only $9.95!* "That comes with all-you-can-eat fries?"

"You have to finish what you have before I bring more." Carol wrote on her pad as she talked. "And what about you?"

"Um." It took me a second to realize she was talking to me. "I'll have the teriyaki chicken sandwich." It cost less than the burger, and the red star next to it said, *Low in Fat!*

"And to drink?"

"Just water."

Joey searched the menu. "The Cokes have free refills?"

"Free refills on pop and coffee."

"Give me a Coke, then." He pointed to a section at the bottom of the menu. "And how does this free birthday meal work? Do we have to tell you when we order that it's her birthday?"

For a second, I didn't understand what he was asking. Not until Carol rolled her eyes to me. She sounded annoyed, like I was trying to pull one over on her. "To get the free meal, you have to have a valid ID saying today's your birthday."

"Oh." Heat pulsed in my cheeks. "Okay." I opened my purse, started digging around. Stupid! Here I was worried about mooching, but he wasn't even paying for my meal.

I found my billfold and opened it. A loose rose petal fell into my lap like a letter from the sky: *He brought you a rose! You're not a cheap date!*

But I was, apparently. He probably picked up the rose while paying for his cigarettes at the gas station. I brushed the petal to the floor and handed over my license.

Carol squinted at it.

"So her meal's free?" Joey asked.

"Anything under ten bucks." She handed back my license, her voice softening. "You still got two bucks," she told me. "You can get a pop instead of water."

"That's okay." I lowered my head, knowing the hurt had settled on my face.

Carol took our menus and hurried off. Joey leaned across the booth. "You think I'm cheap, don't you?"

I bit my lip, shrugged. "Free is free."

"You're disappointed."

"No."

"Just so you know? I'm trying to save up. I found this apartment I need to put a deposit on." He leaned back in the booth. "For my dad and me."

I glanced up. So he was supporting his dad?

"The bank foreclosed on our house after Mom went to prison. My uncle's letting us use his address so Child Protective Services doesn't think I'm homeless. But we're not really living there. You've seen where we're staying."

The storage room in his uncle's bar. I thought about taking his hand, to let him know how bad I felt. But maybe he'd see that as too touchy-feely. "That sucks," I said.

"So that's why I'm trying to save money."

"Can't your dad work?"

Joey barked a laugh. "You've seen him, right? He's no better than my mom. The only difference is he hasn't shot anyone yet."

I swallowed. What do you say to something like that?

He leaned closer, took my hand, looked me in the eye. "I wanted to take you somewhere nice, but this was the best I could do."

"It's fine." He didn't need to apologize. "It's great."

Carol came back, laying down little napkins for our drinks. I liked how the straws were already in them with a bit of wrapper on top to keep them sanitary. I liked that my water came with a lemon wedge even though I hadn't asked for one.

While Joey drained half his Coke, I squeezed the lemon into my water and watched the seeds sink to the bottom. I thought about the red rose sitting in Joey's car, the CD of mood music in my purse. He was trying to make things special for me.

"What?" Joey asked. "Why are you smiling?"

"Was I?" I took a sip of my lemon-flavored water. "I guess you caught me."

CHAPTER 20

Joey's uncle Johnny lived in an old house on the east side of Decatur, the kind of neighborhood with cracked sidewalks and scraggly grass. The screened-in porch was missing half its screens. Joey unlocked the door and pushed it open.

The house was dark and silent. As my eyes adjusted, I made out the shadowy outlines of a couch and a recliner, a coffee table splattered with newspapers and remote controls. A smell like rotting fruit, but sourer.

"Smells like piss," Joey said. "Sorry about that."

A wave of goose bumps prickled my skin. I hugged myself, nervous, a little scared, too. I hadn't forgotten what I'd promised him.

"You okay?" Joey asked.

I nodded. "Just cold."

"Come on." He led me through the dark living room to the kitchen and flipped on the light. The fluorescent bulbs flickered before settling into a muffled gloom.

"You can sit down." He pointed to the card table against the wall.

"Thanks." The table wobbled when I put my elbow on it.

Joey opened the refrigerator and pulled out a carton of orange juice. "Ever had a screwdriver?"

"Huh-uh."

"Vodka and orange juice. You hardly taste the vodka." He grabbed two glasses from the cupboard and blew in them before filling them with ice from the freezer.

I couldn't stop shivering. It didn't help that I had to use the bathroom. "Um," I said. "Do you have a bathroom?" Stupid question. What house didn't have a bathroom?

"Down the hallway." He pointed. "First door on the left."

The bathroom door was closed. Something scratched at it from the inside. Something whimpered.

"I think there's a dog in here!" I called.

"His name's Po'Boy," he called back. "Try not to let him out."

The dog barked once. Maybe he recognized his name.

When I cracked open the door, the heavy urine smell hit me in the face like a wet snowball. A big black nose poked its way out of the gap. I blocked the opening with my body and slid inside.

The dog was a black lab. He wagged his tail and stuck his nose in my crotch. I pushed his muzzle away, letting him sniff my hand and lick my fingers. "Hey, Po'Boy," I whispered. "Good boy."

The bathtub was streaked with yellowish-orange stains, some dry, some still wet. Kibbles of dog food crunched under my feet. The water bowl was almost empty. I rinsed it out in the sink and refilled it.

The sickly sweet stench wasn't helping my nervous stomach. I used the toilet as fast as I could, patting Po'Boy's head and scratching behind his ears to keep him from sniffing me. "Good boy," I kept saying. "Good Po'Boy."

When I got back to the kitchen, Joey had the CD out of my purse. "Hope you don't mind," he said. "It was right on top."

I must have left my purse unzipped. "Should we let the dog out?" I said. "We could take him for a quick walk."

"I'm supposed to keep him locked up." Joey handed me a glass of what looked like orange juice on ice. "He tears up the house when he's out."

It seemed cruel to me, to keep a dog penned up all day, but what did I know about dogs? I'd had a dog when I was six. I barely remembered him, but I did remember how I came home from school one day and he didn't come running to greet me. I never saw him again. Mom and Dad had said he ran away.

"Taste it," Joey said. "Tell me what you think."

I imagined I could smell the vodka. Or maybe it was the lingering pee smell. I took a sip. He was right. I could hardly taste the alcohol. I drank again, felt my shoulders relaxing with every sip.

"You like it?" he asked.

"It's good."

He eyed my glass. "I'll be right back. Drink up."

He took the CD to the living room, and I sipped my screwdriver. I imagined I could feel the alcohol soaking into my flesh, draining away all the tension in my muscles. Then the music started. A slow buildup of guitar and drums flowing from what must have been an awesome stereo system. The swell of the music reminded me of being lost, of longing for something, or someone. I closed my eyes. A wave of goose bumps trailed up my neck.

"You like it?"

I opened my eyes. Joey was smiling down at me.

"Sadie was right. It's good."

He took my glass. "Let me get you another drink."

The second screwdriver tasted stronger than the first, but I didn't mind. Suddenly I felt very chatty.

"So how old are you?" I asked. "My mom wondered how old you were, and I couldn't tell her because I don't know. I mean, I know you're in high school, but—"

"Would you believe me if I said I was twenty-two?"

"No." It took me a second to figure out why I didn't believe that. Because he'd talked with Sadie about quitting school. And he was afraid of living with foster parents. Twenty-two-year-olds didn't live with foster parents.

"Good," he said. "'Cause I'm seventeen, same as you. Remember the fake ID I showed you?"

"I'm eighteen," I reminded him.

"An older woman."

"With a lot less experience."

He smiled with one side of his mouth. "We can fix that."

"Oh yeah?" The words slipped out like I'd been practicing cool all my life.

He gripped the back of my neck, pulled my head toward his. Then he kissed me, his tongue gliding over my bottom lip.

"You taste good," I murmured. Had I just said that?

"How're you feeling?" he asked. "Still cold?"

"Huh-uh."

He stood up. "Finish your drink. I'll be right back."

He disappeared into another part of the house. I heard a door opening and closing. Po'Boy barked three times. Then he was quiet. Poor dog.

I drank, sucking the vodka from the ice cubes. *Buzzed*. That was the word I'd heard everyone say. *I'm buzzed*. Buzzed was a good way to describe it. Everything vibrated with a little more intensity.

Joey came back and leaned in the doorway. "You want to try something cool?"

"Sure." Maybe.

He laid a pill on the table. "It's safe."

I stared at it. White and small. Tiny even. "Safe?"

"As in, it wasn't made in someone's trailer. You know what you're getting. Just a little high. A little—" He cut himself off. "You'll like it."

"That's okay." I shook my head. Would he be mad at me for saying no?

"You sure?"

I bit my lip. "It's not really my thing."

He swept the pill off the table and popped it in his mouth. "You don't mind, do you?"

"Huh-uh."

"Maybe you'll try it next time when you see what it does."

Next time. He was talking about a next time.

"Come with me." He held out his hand to pull me up. "Since you're into art, I want to show you something."

I felt a little dizzy as I stood up, but his hand on my arm steadied me.

"It's in my uncle's bedroom. I always thought it was pretty cool."

I followed him to the bedroom at the end of the hallway. Above the bed was a wall poster of Salvador Dalí's *The Persistence of Memory*, with its melting clocks and strange, mutated creature in the center. The creature was supposedly some kind of self-portrait.

Joey waved at the painting. "It's cool, right?"

"Very cool."

Joey grinned. "One time I stared at this thing for, like, five minutes. Come here for a second." He climbed up to stand on the bed so his face was at eye level with the poster.

I scrambled up after him.

"Careful." He put his hand on my back. "Look at this." He pointed to the hands on the different clocks. "They all show different times."

"Like for different memories." All the times I'd seen this painting, and I'd never noticed that. I liked how Dalí's memories seemed warped.

Our eyes met. A buzzy thrill spiraled through my core.

Joey traced the outline of my jaw. "I tricked you in here, you know."

"It was a good trick."

"So now that we're here . . ." He drew me down so we were kneeling on the bed.

"Your uncle won't come home?"

"He's closing the bar."

I got lost, then, while Sadie's music caressed my senses. Joey's mouth against mine, his tongue, the hunger of it. His body grinding against mine, his need. We didn't move apart to undress, just groped and gasped while first his shirt came off, then my sweater and lacy black bra. They were my hands groping at his zipper. *My* hands pulling down his jeans.

He tugged up my skirt and peeled down my tights and underwear till they sagged at my knees. His hips toggled my legs apart. At the last second, I thought the word *condom*, but interrupting things in that moment would have been so typically me in all my awkward glory. He hovered over me, his attention focused on steering himself to the right place. He pushed. I gasped. And then the dog barked.

And didn't stop. Po'Boy's deep woofs vibrated the walls. Joey kept going. I bit my lip and gripped the edges of the bed. It didn't hurt exactly, but I couldn't concentrate on anything except Po'Boy. The barking turned to howling, and that's when Joey pulled out.

"Shit," he gasped. "Stupid fucking dog."

Was he finished? I didn't think he'd finished. "We forgot a condom" was all I could think to say.

"Yeah." He was still breathing hard.

My skirt was bunched up at the waist. I pulled it down. "I think he's lonely."

Joey's jaw tightened. He dropped his chin to his chest and looked down at himself. "Maybe you can quiet him down. He doesn't like me."

I found my sweater and pulled it on. Stripped off my tights and underwear but left my skirt on. "Be right back," I said.

Po'Boy almost knocked me over making his escape. That's when I caught myself in the mirror. Used up, like a dirty dishrag. I wet my fingers and rubbed at the black smears under my eyes. I left the bathroom door open so Po'Boy could get a drink if he got thirsty.

When I got back to the bedroom, Joey was digging in the front pocket of his jeans, completely naked. He looked better in my fantasies, but this was real life. Life wasn't perfect. Then I felt something wet trickle down my thigh. Blood?

Joey held up a little foil package in the shape of a square. "Your condom."

Would he be grossed out if he saw me bleeding? "Can I turn off the light?"

"Go ahead."

I flipped the switch. "Where are you?" I whispered.

He didn't answer, but I followed the rustle of the condom wrapper and groped my way toward him.

• • •

When it was over, he lay on top of me for a few seconds, his face buried in my neck. My hip joints hurt from his weight pressing on me. It felt good when he rolled away, but I wanted him to stay. I wanted to hold his hand. I wanted it to feel special.

We lay side by side. His chest moved up and down as he caught his breath. He reached down, past his stomach. I heard a wet, squelching noise. I was glad for the darkness.

He sat up, slid his feet to the floor. "Be back in a minute."

When he opened the door, a shaft of light showed me the flattened spill of my breasts. I covered myself with the blanket, felt the tacky wetness between my legs. Would I ruin the moment if I got up to clean myself?

He was gone for a long time. I heard water running. When he came back, he stood in the doorway with a towel around his waist. I pulled the blanket to my chest.

"You look tired," he said. "I'll take you home."

I curled the blanket around my fists and glanced at the clock beside the bed. *10:09.* I'd officially turned eighteen an hour ago. Should I tell him that?

His phone rang from the pocket of his jeans. He pulled it out, answered it.

"Hey . . . Yeah, I know." He glanced at the clock. "Okay. No problem." He hung up.

We looked at each other. He didn't have to say it.

"I'll get dressed," I said.

He was already pulling on his jeans.

I picked up my scattered clothes, headed to the bathroom. I heard Po'Boy scrambling around on the other side of the door and realized Joey must have penned him up again. The dog whined when I came in, stuck his nose between my legs.

I pushed him away. "Bad dog."

He looked at me, wagging his tail.

I grabbed a wad of toilet paper and propped one leg on the toilet to clean myself. Disgusting. The heavy pee odor turned my stomach, and the dog wouldn't leave me alone. He tried to lick my hands while I wiped up blood, and when I shoved him away, he whimpered but came right back and tried to sniff me.

"Stop!" I hissed, but he didn't listen. He whined and panted and nosed for my crotch. Finally, I rapped him on the nose— once, twice—hard enough that he cringed and backed away.

CHAPTER 21

The next day at school, I was hiding out in the girls' restroom to eat lunch when my cell phone rang. Joey had said he'd call, but it wasn't Joey. It was Dad's lawyer calling me back. I'd left another message for her that morning.

"Hello?"

"Tera, it's Charlotte Gross."

I held my breath, my hand tightening around the phone.

"I got your messages," she said. "They can't find you in the system because your dad hasn't put you on the approved visitors' list."

"But why not? He knows when my birthday is. He knows when I'm allowed to visit him."

"I don't know. You'll have to talk to him."

"But I can't, not until he puts me on the list. Tell him, please."

"I will."

This didn't make sense. Why didn't he want to talk to me? I gave up Paris for him, and now he didn't want to talk to me?

"I had another reason for calling," she said. "We've had time to examine the evidence. Can you come to my office this afternoon?"

"Um, sure." She was making me nervous. "Is something wrong?"

"I can fit you in today at two-thirty."

I'd have to skip Art, but maybe I could get Mr. Stewart's permission. "Okay," I said. I noticed how she hadn't answered my question.

"I'll see you then." She hung up.

I threw away the rest of my lunch and went to find Mr. Stewart. If he saw how worried I was—if I explained how important it was that I see the lawyer—he'd excuse me so I wouldn't get in trouble for skipping again.

I almost ran into Mr. Stewart coming out of the faculty lounge, right on the heels of Principal Meyer. Mr. Stewart kept walking even though I knew he saw me. I started to go after him, but Principal Meyer blocked my path. He smiled and looked down at me.

"Hello, Tera."

I murmured a hello. Since when did the principal stop to chat?

"How are you holding up?" He cleared his throat. "What I mean is, how are you doing?"

"Fine." I glanced behind him. Mr. Stewart was getting lost in the crowd of students.

"Are you sure? You seem distracted."

"Sorry. I just really need to talk to Mr. Stewart."

He frowned and looked behind him to where Mr. Stewart was disappearing down the hallway. "Mordecai!" he called.

Hearing his name, Mr. Stewart stopped in his tracks.

Principal Meyer's chuckle sounded forced. "Let's make sure he doesn't get away."

I followed the principal to where Mr. Stewart had backed himself against the wall. He kept his head down, didn't look at me, almost like he didn't want to be seen with me. Maybe Principal Meyer yelled at him for playing favorites.

Principal Meyer smoothed his tie. "This young lady needs to talk to you."

"Of course," he murmured.

"But stop by my office later," Principal Meyer told him. "We'll finish our conversation."

Mr. Stewart watched him go. "What is it, Tera?"

Was he mad at me for something? Is that why he wouldn't look at me? I was the one who should've been mad at him, for refusing to help bail out my dad, for calling my drawings *trite*.

I shifted my backpack to the other shoulder. "My dad's lawyer wants me to come by this afternoon."

"And?"

"So I have to miss class."

Kids brushed past me. Someone bumped me.

"Is your mom excusing this absence?"

"Well, no. I haven't told her I'm seeing the lawyer."

"Then I still have to mark you absent."

"But then I'll get detention." I couldn't deal with that right now. I had enough to deal with.

"I can't play favorites, Tera." He looked at his watch. "I have to go."

"Yeah, sure," I said as he walked away. "Sorry to keep you."

• • •

I caught the bus to the lawyer's office, so nervous that I felt sick. Charlotte Gross had said she'd examined the evidence. I wanted so badly to hear good news.

She was ready to see me as soon as I got there. She wore a gray pantsuit and white blouse with lots of ruffles. A thick gold bracelet dangled from her wrist.

"Tera." Her handshake was firm. "So nice to see you again."

"You, too."

"Please have a seat."

I perched on the edge of a cushy chair in front of her desk and clenched my hands in front of me. The tighter I clenched, the easier it was to breathe.

"So how have you been?" she asked.

"Fine." I swallowed. Enough with the chitchat.

"I spoke with your father about the allegations, and he gave me permission to speak to you."

"Okay." That was a good sign. He had nothing to hide.

"Let's start at the beginning," she said. "Your father is being charged with possession of child pornography, which has a minimum sentence of five years for each count."

I nodded. This was nothing new.

"You mentioned to me in our previous meeting that you thought a sketch they found was drawn by you."

"To practice," I said.

"To practice." She nodded. "But the fact remains that the drawing was in your father's possession. Remember, he's not being accused of drawing it; he's being accused of possessing it. Do you understand the difference?"

"Yes, but the drawing was in the trash—not really in his possession."

"It was in his office."

"But—"

"There's good news here. The prosecution has to prove to a jury that a sketch is obscene. Otherwise, it's protected under the First Amendment." Her voice softened. "I saw what you drew, Tera, and it's my strong belief that a jury will fail to find it obscene."

I tried to make sense of her words. My drawing wasn't the problem. But something else was?

"I don't believe the prosecution will try to prove it's pornographic because any reasonable jury would find that it does *not* portray sexual conduct in a patently offensive way."

"Okay." That sounded like good news, but somehow it wasn't. "What—"

"Let me finish. I just want to stress that none of this is your fault. You understand that, right?"

"Yes." I almost whispered it. The other shoe was about to drop. I could feel it.

"Good." She straightened a ruffle on her blouse. "You also need to know that the police found photos and some digital art on his computer. The images had been deleted, but they were still present on his hard drive."

A tiny spark of panic flared in my chest. "What are you saying?"

"They found child pornography," she said. "Children engaged in sexual acts with adults and other children."

I stared at her. "No," I said. "That can't be right."

"But let me stress." She went on like I hadn't spoken. "This doesn't mean your father is guilty."

I felt blind. The panic I'd been forcing down rose higher, made it hard to breathe. "How could it *not* mean that?"

She spoke softly, calmly. "Sometimes people are not aware they've downloaded pornographic images."

I squinted at her, not daring to hope. "What do you mean?"

"We're not really sure how the images ended up on his computer. We're running a full analysis of his hard drive to find out, but there are a number of ways these kinds of things happen. They could have come from pop-up advertisements on pornography sites. Or maybe he downloaded adult pornography, but it was bundled with pornographic images of children."

So what was she saying? That the photos got on his computer by accident?

She was still talking. "Like any reasonable person, he tried to delete the offensive images once he discovered what he had downloaded. But he didn't realize the images remained on his hard drive, just waiting to implicate him."

I felt numb as I studied her through glassy eyes. The hotshot lawyer with her fancy pen and gold bracelet. So sure of herself. "Is that what really happened?" I asked.

Her lips curved up in a smile. She tapped her pen against her chin. "That's what we're going to prove."

CHAPTER 22

Before I left her office, Charlotte Gross told me she'd won several cases where her client had accidentally downloaded child pornography. It could happen to anyone, she said. She told me not to worry, that everything would work out the way it was supposed to.

It was almost five o'clock by the time I got home from the lawyer's. Still no call from Joey. I came in through the kitchen. Mom was watching TV in the living room and didn't look up. It seemed she hadn't noticed I was late coming home from school.

The phone in the kitchen rang. The word *attorney* popped up in the caller ID. I answered it before Mom could pick it up.

"Hello?"

A man's voice. He sounded old. "May I speak to Tera Waters?"

"This is Tera."

"Miss Waters, my name is Herman Liebowitz. I'm the lead prosecutor in your father's case."

My mind whirled to catch up. This was the lawyer going *against* my dad.

"I'm calling to introduce myself," he said.

Mom chose that moment to wander into the kitchen.

"Okay," I said into the phone. But what was this about? Why was he calling me?

"I'd like to invite you to stop by my office so we can talk. Are you free tomorrow?"

Did he think I was on his side? Did he think I had some kind of dirt on my dad? "I can't," I said. "I have school."

Mom tapped my arm. "Who is it?"

"Perhaps you could stop by my office after school. Or we could meet on Saturday, if you prefer."

"I'm sorry," I said. "But I don't know what this is about."

"Well, it's about your father's case."

Could he be more vague? "Just so you know?" I said. "*I'm* the one who hired my dad's lawyer. So if you're thinking I want to help you, you need to come up with another plan."

A pause. "That's fine, Miss Waters. I simply wanted to introduce myself. Will you take down my name and number?"

"My dad didn't do anything wrong," I said.

"Well, maybe you can tell me about that."

"I'm telling you now."

"Take down my name and number, Miss Waters. You may find yourself needing to contact me."

"Fine." I grabbed a pencil from my backpack and flipped open a notebook. "Go ahead."

Mom looked over my shoulder as I scribbled down his information. "I got it," I said. "I have to go now." I hung up, suddenly exhausted.

Mom sank into a kitchen chair. "I told him not to call you."

"What are you talking about?"

"He's the prosecuting attorney. I already talked to him. He wanted to talk to you, but I told him to leave you out of it. You're too young to get involved."

"I'm eighteen," I snapped.

"Don't you think I know that by now?"

"So what did you tell him, Mom?" I shoved my notebook into my backpack and zipped it up. "What did you tell this Herman Liebowitz guy?"

"I told him the truth."

The truth as she saw it. She'd said she found "something" on Dad's computer, and now I knew what that something was.

I pictured Charlotte Gross leaning back in her chair. Charlotte Gross tapping her pen on her chin. She'd said we could build a defense. That's what she'd said, and I wanted so badly to believe it. Dad couldn't have known the pictures were there until Mom found them. And like any reasonable person, he'd tried to delete them.

"It's all circumstantial," I said. "Whatever you found." I wasn't sure if it was circumstantial or not—I wasn't even sure what *circumstantial* meant—but Dad's lawyer thought we could make a case, so the evidence must not have been clear-cut.

I felt Mom's eyes on me. I couldn't look at her. Not if I wanted to keep believing Dad was innocent. Instead, I fiddled with the zipper on my backpack.

"I'm worried about you," she said.

"Don't be. I'm fine."

"The lawyers on both sides . . . They'll ask questions."

And whose fault is that? I wanted to scream. *Who started this whole thing by calling the police?* But I didn't say that. Instead, I lifted my chin and made myself look her in the eye. "I can handle it."

• • •

Eight days until the contest deadline.

After school the next day, I dragged all my paints and brushes back down to Dad's studio. Maybe something down there would inspire me. I stood before a blank canvas and tried not to think how it had been two days since I'd seen Joey on my birthday. Two days since I'd had *sex* with him and still he hadn't called.

Instead, I thought about that rainy day when I saw my reflection in the bus window—a girl excited to see a boy at work because he'd flirted with her, a girl who didn't know about the photos on her dad's computer. The outside world felt desperate and gray, but the girl had hope, so her tiny smile lit up the bus.

I squeezed yellow paint onto my palette, mixed it with purple to form a cool, stony gray. I took a breath, closed my eyes to shut out the world. Then I dipped my brush and began to paint. The picture in my mind spread across the canvas.

But Dad's shadow loomed. I was in *his* studio, and the canvas before me was *his* canvas. The paintbrush in my hand was a birthday gift from him.

It was almost midnight when I stepped back to look at what I'd done. My girl on the bus stared at her reflection in the rain-streaked window, her face pale and shadowy gray. The other riders on the bus wore muted yellows, greens, and blues. They talked, smiled, pointed. But my girl sat alone, wrapped in a coarse coat the color of storm clouds. Her dark hair framed her face in damp strands. Only her smile gave off any kind of color, a bright rosy pink. I wanted the smile to light up the girl's face, but instead it looked pasted on. False.

Maybe it was the lighting. Maybe after I saw Joey at work in a few days, I'd know how to fix it.

● ● ●

I tried to finish my Trig homework on the school bus the next morning, but the ride was so bouncy that I couldn't concentrate. Then my phone rang. My pencil rolled off the seat as I dug the phone out of my purse.

Please let it be Joey, I thought. But it wasn't. It was Dad's lawyer. I looked around to make sure no one on the bus could overhear. The closest person was Josh Henderson, sitting two seats in front of me with headphones over his ears.

I flipped open my phone, made sure to speak softly. "Hello?"

"Tera, it's Charlotte Gross." A pause. "Your dad wanted me to give you a message."

"Okay." I held my breath, waiting.

"He wanted me to tell you that he put you on his visitors' list. So you shouldn't have any problems going to see him."

"That's great!" Sudden relief made my voice too loud. I glanced over at Josh, but he seemed engrossed in something on his phone.

"Did he say anything else?" I asked. "Is there any news on the case?"

"Nothing I can talk about right now. I have to go."

As usual, her goodbye was abrupt, bordering on rude, but I didn't care. I searched my phone until I found the number for the jail. Josh still had his headphones on, so I went ahead and dialed it.

It took a minute to get through the automated voice system. By that time, Lindsay Price and her sister Molly were on the bus, too. But they always sat in the first seat. There was no way they could overhear.

The man at the jail who answered sounded like the same man I'd talked to before.

"I need to schedule a visit with my dad," I told him. "My name's Tera Waters. W-A-T-E-R-S. My dad's name is Timothy Waters."

I stared at my Trig book as he looked me up in his computer.

"Okay," he said. "When would you like to come in?"

Relief almost made me smile. "Tonight?"

"His cell block isn't allowed visitors on Wednesday evening. You can come Tuesday, Wednesday, or Friday during the day. Monday or Thursday evening. Saturday or Sunday, nine to eight."

I had to work on Thursday, and I had school on Friday. "I'll come Saturday," I said. "Can I come in the morning?"

"Make it ten o'clock."

I closed my phone and bowed my head, so relieved that my chest hurt. Now Dad could explain to me how those photos had ended up on his computer, and I'd know for sure he was innocent. Now I could see how he looked, how he was holding up. And he could thank me for helping him. I didn't realize until that moment how much I needed his gratitude.

CHAPTER 23

Joey still hadn't called by Thursday, so on the bus to work, I thought of what I'd do when I saw him. I'd act casual, like we were friends. I'd ask him about his band, how long it had been since he played a gig, whether he played any instruments other than bass.

By the time I clocked in, I thought I was ready to see him. I thought I was ready to talk to him. But when I saw him coming out of the walk-in, my throat closed up. I kept on toward the dining room like I hadn't seen him.

He smiled and put out his hand to stop me. "Hey, I didn't know you worked tonight."

And yet, I knew his entire schedule. How pathetic was that? I made myself shrug. "I'm here all evening."

Mr. Barnes came hustling out of his office, straightening his tie. "Joey, did you mix up that extra pizza dough?"

"Yeah, it's in the walk-in."

Mr. Barnes turned to me. "You should make good tips. There's some kind of comic or science-fiction convention going on at the Marriott. It starts tonight."

"A geek con," Joey said. "People walking around in Star Wars costumes."

"It's Adventure-Con," I said. I knew all about Adventure-Con. When Dad was trying to break into the comic-book business, he'd bring his portfolio to Adventure-Con to show it to the editors and agents.

"You're into all that?" Joey asked me.

Would he like me less if I was? I shrugged. "Not really."

"I remember now," said Mr. Barnes. "Your dad's a comic-book artist. Is he over there signing autographs? Tell him to send people to Papa Geppetto's for dinner."

"Sure, okay."

Joey raised his eyebrows at me. Maybe he thought I had lied when I said my dad was in jail.

I leaned closer, so only Joey could hear. "No one here knows about my dad."

He shrugged. "That's cool."

At least we were talking. That night of my birthday—the night I'd had sex with him—I lay in bed and imagined what it would be like to work with him. I pictured us smiling at each other from across the room, exchanging knowing glances, maybe sneaking off to the back room to kiss. Maybe it was normal for guys to act like nothing had changed after you slept together. Maybe it didn't mean anything that he hadn't called.

Sadie worked the dining room with me, and a tall Asian guy I'd never met worked in the kitchen with Joey. He looked about my age and had a sprinkling of acne on his cheeks.

Dinner was crazy busy. Most everyone who came in wore a costume—Star Trek, Star Wars, fairies, anime. They looked like they were having fun. If Dad hadn't been in jail, I would have asked if they'd heard of Timothy Waters, the guy who drew the *After End* series of graphic novels. I could have bragged how he was my dad.

Finally, the dining room cleared out except for one table of guys wearing superhero costumes. Sadie and I took a break behind the server station where we could keep an eye on the floor.

"How'd you do?" she asked me. "I cleared a hundred bucks."

Then Joey was beside me, filling a glass with ice. I forgot Sadie's question when his arm brushed mine. Did he want to talk to me? The tall Asian guy joined us, too. *Cam*, his nametag said. Cam smiled an apology when he reached in front of me for a glass.

Joey leaned against the counter next to me, but his eyes were on Sadie. A twinge of jealousy made me look away as he tugged one of the strings of her smock. I sipped my drink, trying to pretend it didn't bother me.

"Hey, Sadie," he said. "I dare you go out there and tell those guys how sexy they look in their tights."

She rolled her eyes and popped a piece of ice into her mouth. "Give me twenty bucks and I will."

"They'll pay *you*," Joey said. "You know they're virgins. Twenty bucks is a bargain if you take them out back."

She punched him in the arm. "What do I look like?"

Joey grinned and rubbed his arm. "You really want me to answer that?"

She laughed and punched him again.

I dumped my ice in the sink. The sound helped drown out their laughter. From the corner of my eye, I caught the tall Asian guy watching me. He walked up and stuck out his hand. "I'm Cam, by the way."

"Hi." I shook his hand. "I'm Tera."

Cam started to say something, but Joey's laughter cut him off.

"Hey, Tera, *you* should go out there," Joey said. "Tell them your dad's a comic-book artist and see what they do. They'll probably fall down and worship you."

Cam looked up from filling his glass with ice. "Your dad's a comic-book artist?"

I clenched my arms at the elbows, tried to smile. "It's not a big deal."

"Is he at the convention? Maybe I could get his autograph."

"I . . ." I looked down, felt Joey's eyes on me.

"Is your dad really an artist?" Sadie asked. "Is he famous?"

"Not really. I mean, he's an artist and he's sort of famous. It depends on who you talk to."

"What's his name?" Cam asked. "I might have some of his stuff."

I opened my mouth to say his name. *Timothy Waters*. But I couldn't get the words out. Cam's eyes darted to Sadie, to Joey, back to me.

I kneeled down and rummaged under the sink for a clean rag, any excuse to hide my face. I heard them murmuring. I heard Sadie tell them to give me some space. When I heard them walk away, I stood.

Joey was still there, topping off a beer from the tap. He sipped off the foam. "You okay?"

I shrugged.

Setting down his beer, he moved in close and wrapped his arms around my waist. "I can make you okay," he said. "I can make you very, very okay."

His body pressed into mine. Warm. Hard. Good.

"Do you want that?" he whispered.

I looked into his eyes. Hazel, the pupils black and large. I nodded.

His smile was gentle, teasing. "Let me hear you say it."

"I want that."

"Excellent." The growl in his voice made me shiver. "I'll drive you home tonight."

• • •

I finished my side-work, but I had to wait on Joey, so I took a seat in one of the empty booths to count my tip money. I liked the smell of the bills, like pages in a book. Like a fresh canvas.

"Tera?" The booth creaked as Cam sat across from me. "I just wanted to say I'm sorry about your dad."

My jaw tightened, made it hard to talk without sounding rude. "What do you mean?"

"Just that . . . He's in jail. I'm sorry. I didn't know."

And now he did. Now I wasn't Tera who could be anybody. Now I was Tera whose dad was in jail.

For child pornography. The thought wormed its way to the front of my brain. I forced it back. My dad was innocent.

"If I'd known," he said, "I wouldn't have asked about an autograph."

"Joey told you?" It had to have been him. He was the only one who knew.

"I didn't believe it at first," Cam said. "I have some of his graphic novels. He doesn't seem like the type who would do that kind of thing."

That kind of thing. But I'd never told Joey why Dad got arrested. He must have found out on his own. And now Cam knew, too, and now he wouldn't *want* Dad's autograph.

"I'm sorry." Cam winced and rubbed his eyebrow. "I'm making this worse."

"Nothing's been proven." I sounded so sure of myself. "It'll be cleared up in a few months."

I had to believe that. Because if I didn't, that meant I'd given up art school for nothing. And it meant I'd spent my whole life looking up to someone who . . .

I couldn't finish the thought because Dad wasn't like that. He had taken only that photo of me to teach me how to sketch the human form. He didn't realize how much it hurt me, and when he did realize it, he was so, so sorry.

"I should go," Cam said.

As he walked away, I looked down at the pile of tip money on the table, every bill crumpled and dirty. I started straightening the bills, putting them in a neat pile. Whatever mistakes my dad had made, he wasn't a bad person. Whatever it was they thought he did, it wasn't true. Charlotte Gross would prove it wasn't true.

A shadow fell across the table. I didn't have to look up to know who it was. I smelled the cigarette smoke on his clothes.

"You ready?" Joey asked.

I nodded but didn't move to get up. How could he stand there like everything was fine between us, when he'd betrayed me by blabbing to Cam?

"So let's go then."

I let myself sit for another second. I could tell him I'd take the bus. I could tell him how pissed I was. Instead, I swept my tips into a pile and stuffed them into my smock. I stood.

"See you later," Sadie called.

I made myself smile and wave.

The night sky was dusky brown. A clear night. I followed Joey across the parking lot to his car. It smelled like an ashtray. I cracked the window as he pulled out of the parking lot. His stereo blasted, but he didn't turn it down.

"So how'd you do today?" he asked.

I stared straight ahead. "What do you mean?"

"Your tips. I saw you counting them. You had a good day?"

"I guess. I didn't finish counting."

Silence.

"Did you listen to those CDs?" he asked.

"There were a lot to listen to."

"Did you listen to any of them?"

"Um, Sleigh Bells. Vampire Weekend."

"And what'd you think? They kick ass, right?"

"They were okay."

He shook a cigarette from his crumpled pack, lit it. Then he looked at me. "So what's up with you?"

I shrugged, knowing he had no idea he'd done anything wrong. "It's been a long day," I said.

"So you're always this moody after a long day?" He laughed as he blew out smoke. "I should have known you were too good to be true."

Too good to be true? I glanced over to see if he was making fun of me. Smoke from his cigarette floated around his face. He looked serious.

"Sorry," I said. "It's just . . ." I wasn't used to calling people out, but I had to tell him. Otherwise, he wouldn't know he'd done anything wrong. "Something's bugging me."

"Fine." He turned the stereo off. "What is it?"

"You told Cam about my dad."

He scrunched his eyebrows together like he was confused. "I wasn't supposed to tell?"

"Well, no. It was private."

"I didn't think it was a big deal."

"It was private," I said again.

Joey braked suddenly and turned into a strip mall. All the windows in the mall were dark, the lot completely empty. He parked in front of a chiropractor's office and twisted in his seat to look at me.

"Listen, I'm sorry, okay? If I'd known it was a secret, I never would've said anything. It's just, he was Googling your dad on his phone. So I told him what I knew—before he could read whatever shit is floating around out there about him."

"What do you mean? There's, like, a news story about him?"

He shrugged. "It just said he got arrested for kiddie porn. And then a bunch of people responded to it. Fans, I guess. Or former fans."

So all those people who would have asked for his autograph . . . They wouldn't be asking anymore. I curled my hands against my stomach and stared out the front window. I couldn't imagine what Dad was feeling. All that work he'd put into becoming an artist people recognized. And now they'd want nothing to do with him.

Joey crushed out his cigarette in the ashtray. "So your dad's a perv. I didn't think it was a big deal."

"It's not like that," I said. "He hasn't had a trial."

"Whatever you say." Joey took my hand, uncurled my fingers, squeezed. "I'm sorry, okay?"

"Okay."

"Seriously. I'm really sorry." His face was shadowed in darkness, but the glow from the dashboard console reflected off his eyes, made them look golden. "You forgive me?"

Did I? I kept forgetting how he didn't think it was a big deal that his mom was in prison for murder. So of course he wouldn't think this thing with my dad was a big deal either.

I smiled a little. "I forgive you."

He turned off the car. "Let me make it up to you."

The seat squeaked as he leaned in. His lips pressed into mine, warm and urgent. One of his hands slid around my back, then up my waist to my chest. His mouth found my neck while his other hand undid the buttons on my uniform blouse. He pulled up my bra, not bothering with the clasp. My breasts hung there, squished and bare.

"I want you so bad," Joey murmured. "Tell me you want me, too."

"I do. I want you." Which was true, but the words felt awkward, silly. Especially with my breasts hanging beneath my bra.

He leaned back to unbuckle his belt. "Take off your pants."

"In the car?"

"No one will see."

"But . . ."

He pulled a condom from his jeans pocket. "See? Everything's fine. And I need you. Right now." He tugged his pants down his hips.

I did what he told me. I unbuttoned my uniform pants, peeled them down. He tugged at my underwear and pulled them down, too. By then, he wasn't looking at me. By then, he was rolling on the condom. So he didn't see how clumsy I looked getting undressed. Like a wounded spider, legs cramped and wiggling.

He edged on top of me, his weight pushing me back. My head pressed against the passenger door, my neck bent and strained.

This time it hurt more, but it was over quick. When he was done, he stayed on top of me, his breath warming my neck. I laid my hands across his sweaty back, counted his heartbeats against my chest. His breath felt heavy. *He* felt heavy.

When I got to twenty beats and he still hadn't moved, I couldn't help wondering: Was this what it felt like to be close to someone?

• • •

Joey and I didn't talk the whole ride home. He looked over and smiled once, and then he went back to smoking and listening to his music. Was he done with me, then? Was I still "too good to be true"?

He parked the car in front of my house and tossed his cigarette out the open window. "So my uncle's having a party tomorrow night."

My heart pounded. I sat very still.

"You want to go?"

"Sure." My voice sounded distant. Was that *me* sounding so laid back?

"I'll pick you up around nine."

"Okay."

"And don't eat before you come."

So dinner and a party. Dessert, too, I was guessing. I knew how Joey liked his dessert.

CHAPTER 24

Five days until the contest deadline.

I'd left my *Girl on a Bus* painting sitting in Dad's studio, still not sure if it was good enough for the contest. The girl in the painting was supposed to be smiling as she thought about her boyfriend, but I was worried that her smile looked too much like moustache graffiti.

So after Joey dropped me off, I crept downstairs to look at it with fresh eyes. The girl in the painting stared at herself in the rain-streaked window, her tiny smile vivid against the muted colors of her surroundings. Not moustache graffiti, I decided. The brightness of her smile made a statement. She felt happy and sad at the same time.

Mom's voice called down from the top of the stairs. "Tera? Is that you?"

"Yeah, it's me. I just got home."

The stairs creaked as she made her way down. "What are you doing? Are you painting?"

"Just looking," I said.

"At what?"

I pointed to *Girl on a Bus*, still on the easel.

"Wow," she said. "It's good."

"Good enough to win ten thousand dollars?"

She folded her arms. "You're asking me? I'm not the artist."

"I know. I just wanted your opinion."

"Show it to your art teacher. He'll know."

But I didn't want to show it to Mr. Stewart, not with him acting like I had some kind of plague. "There's no time," I lied. "I have to send it out."

"Then send it out. What are you waiting for?"

I wasn't sure. Another idea? If something came to me, I could always enter another painting. The contest rules said you could enter up to three. So there was no reason not to send it.

After Mom went upstairs, I found Dad's camera in one of his drawers. I wasn't a photographer, so it took me several tries to get a shot of the painting that didn't have a glare on it. When I was satisfied, I plugged the camera's memory card into my borrowed laptop, filled out the online entry form, and uploaded *Girl on a Bus* to the contest website.

Sending it felt like the first step to getting on with my life.

● ● ●

In World History the next day, Haley squatted beside my desk. Her perfume reminded me of a cloying purple. She hadn't said a word to me since that day when she'd tried to get me in her car. I thought she'd gotten the hint, but apparently not.

I glanced at the clock. One minute until class started.

"Hey," she said. "I have to tell you something." Her eyes strayed to the doorway as her boyfriend, Sam Minoz, strolled into the classroom. He smiled and waved. She waved back.

Smiling and waving. That's what I wanted for Joey and me when we saw each other at work.

"I tried to ask you about it last week," she said. "But you wouldn't talk to me. And then my mom said I shouldn't have any contact with you."

A stab of anger made me sit up straighter. "It's not like I'm contagious," I said. "What does she think will happen if you have contact with me?"

Haley rolled her eyes. "You know how she is."

I didn't, actually. Haley acted like her mom was the most annoying person in the world, but I didn't see it. *Her* mom didn't have mental problems.

Haley was still talking. "So I went ahead and made an appointment to see him."

Did I miss something? I shook my head. "What are you talking about?"

"That lawyer in your dad's case wants to talk to me, but I don't really know what they want." She twisted her hair into a rope. "Do you?"

"You mean Charlotte Gross?" Why would Dad's lawyer want to talk to Haley?

"No. The prosecuting attorney guy. Herman whatever-his-last- name-is."

The bell rang. Mr. Wilson called for everyone to take their seats. Haley stopped playing with her hair and flopped into the seat in front of me. I stared at the back of her head and didn't hear a word of Mr. Wilson's lecture.

I could think of only one reason why Herman Liebowitz would want to talk to the girl who lived across the street. He wanted to find out if Dad had done anything to her.

But Haley had a big mouth. She would have said something if Dad had so much as looked at her funny. I knew for a fact she would have said something.

• • •

Joey picked me up twenty minutes late. He leaned into the steering wheel and cocked a smile as I slid into the car. "You look good."

I smiled back. The screaming guitar on his stereo hurt my ears. The lingering smoke turned my empty stomach. But he was here. Finally.

"Before we get going . . ." He shook a pill from a tiny plastic bag and put it in my hand.

I stared at it. "What is it?"

"X. Ecstasy. You didn't eat, did you? It works best on an empty stomach."

"Um." I tried to give it back. "I don't . . ."

His voice hardened. "You don't want it? You said you'd do it next time."

I didn't remember saying that. Fortunately, I had the perfect excuse to say no. "I have to go to the jail in the morning," I told him. "I'm visiting my dad."

"What time are you going?"

"Ten."

He blew air between his lips. "It'll be out of your system by then. You want to start with half? Then you can see what it does and take the other half later tonight."

I knew if I didn't take it, he'd be angry. And really, what was the harm? Everything I'd heard about it said it was awesome—a designer drug—and it wasn't supposed to be addictive, not like heroin or crack.

"Listen," he said. "I know you've been worried about your dad. This'll help you forget, at least for a while."

I stared at the pill in my palm. Forgetting sounded good. Forgetting sounded like heaven. "I'll do half," I said.

He grinned and took the pill out of my hand. Then he bit off half with his front teeth and chased it down with a swig from his water bottle. Still smiling, he held the other half out to me.

Before I could change my mind, I popped the pill into my mouth, wincing at the chalky, bitter taste. I swallowed it down with the water Joey held out to me. "Are you okay to drive?" I asked.

"Don't worry," he said. "It takes about an hour to start working." He popped another pill into his mouth and washed it down. Then he shifted into Drive.

• • •

It took a half-hour to get to his uncle's house. The whole ride over, I was hyper-aware of my senses, trying to figure out if I felt anything from the ecstasy. So far, nothing. Not even a tingle.

When we got to his uncle's house, two guys with buzz cuts were chasing Po'Boy around the yard. Po'Boy leaped around like a gazelle, barking and wagging his tail. I was glad to see him happy. On the porch, we passed a guy and girl sitting on the steps laughing hysterically. Their arms were covered in tattoos.

Joey waved me toward the door. "Go on in. I need to talk to someone."

I was nervous. I didn't want to be alone with a bunch of strangers. But I didn't want Joey to think I was clingy. So I did what he said. I went inside.

The thrum of techno music swallowed me. A guy with spiky white hair and a mess of piercings crouched in front of the stereo system. Joey's uncle lounged on the couch, rubbing at the tattoo on his neck. An older woman with fingernails like talons nestled against his chest, sucking on a cigarette.

I stood near the door, trying to decide where to go, what to do. Sadie was supposed to be here, but she probably had a bunch of people to talk to.

"Hey!" Joey's uncle threw a cigarette at me. "I don't know you."

"Oh." I pointed outside. "I'm with Joey. I met you the other night."

He squinted at me.

"At your bar. I'm Tera."

He smiled as recognition dawned. "Pink."

"Excuse me?"

"Your wine. I always remember people by their drink."

"Oh." A miniature tornado whirled in my gut. But it wasn't nerves. This tornado felt good.

"There's drinks in the fridge. Help yourself." He winked and sipped from his water bottle.

"Thanks."

I wandered into the kitchen. There were a half-dozen people leaning against the counters, smoking but not talking. Some of them had their eyes closed, their heads bobbing to the music. I glanced around, searching for Sadie, but these people were all older, more like Joey's uncle's age than high-school kids.

"You looking for something?" A man peeled himself from the counter. He was a big guy, broad shoulders and heavy around the middle, like an overweight football player. He had a shaved head, just like Joey's uncle. His grin managed to look silly and lustful at the same time.

I needed to relax. I tried reaching for the buzzy tornado feeling in my stomach, but it wasn't there anymore. Maybe I should take the other half. "I just came to get a drink," I said.

He slumped against the counter. "Well, you don't have to look so scared about it. Liquor's on the counter. Other stuff's in the fridge."

"Thanks." I opened the refrigerator. A box of pink wine sat on the shelf. It had a spigot. I found a plastic cup on the counter and filled it half full.

The man watched me. "So how do you know Johnny?"

Johnny. Joey's uncle. "I'm his nephew's girlfriend," I said. That sounded funny, so I laughed. "I'm Tera."

"*Joey's* girlfriend?"

Was it so surprising? I laughed again. The tornado in my stomach was back, only now it was moving up toward my throat. I wanted to lean my head back and stretch, but I knew how weird that would look. I needed to concentrate on what I was doing. "We just started dating," I said.

"That explains it. So how do you know Joey?"

"We work together." It was getting harder to concentrate. "At Papa Geppetto's." The name sounded funny, but I kept myself from giggling.

"Ah." He sipped from his water bottle and looked around.

"Do you know a girl named Sadie?" I asked. "I can't find her."

"Don't know her," he said. And then he closed his eyes, so I figured he was done talking.

I made my way back to the living room. Was it my imagination, or did my body feel lighter? Almost like my veins were filled with helium. Sadie wasn't there, but Joey crouched beside the couch next to his uncle. I gave him a little wave. He held up a finger. *Wait.*

I sipped my drink. Joey kept massaging his own neck, like he had a crick in it, and his uncle kept smiling. The guy with spiky white hair asked me if I had a cigarette. I told him I didn't smoke. He moved on.

Joey kept talking to his uncle, but I didn't mind. I was having fun just watching everyone. Never in my life had I felt so relaxed, so at ease in my body. I looked around for a wall to lean against. I wanted to stretch like a cat. I wanted to lean my head back and just *feel.*

Joey appeared at my side. He had a huge smile. "Sorry about that. Are you feeling it yet?" He stared at my face. "You are, aren't you?"

I grinned. "I feel amazing."

"You want to take the other half?"

I did, but I was scared, too. What I was feeling felt *really* good, and I didn't want to ruin it by taking too much.

Someone turned off the lights and cranked up the music. Thumping bass rattled the wall. The room erupted in cheers. A scattering of glow sticks jerked around in dizzying patterns, cutting the dark with their neon trails of light.

I had to yell to be heard over the music. It was hard to take my eyes off the twirling glow sticks. "Maybe later," I said.

One of the dancers in the middle of the room bumped into me. Two people huddled under a blanket on the recliner. I couldn't see their faces, but they were obviously making out. The woman with the talon fingernails sat on the floor by the coffee table, rolling a joint. I had a sudden flash of what this scene must look like to someone from the outside. Someone like my mom. A total den of iniquity. So what? I was having fun.

Joey took my hand and led me to the couch. His uncle Johnny moved over to make room for us. I flopped down between them, leaned my head back, and smiled.

"Someone's feeling good," Johnny said.

Why hadn't I done this before? "It's my first time," I announced.

Johnny laughed. I saw the look he exchanged with Joey, but I wasn't sure what it meant, and I didn't care.

I rubbed Joey's leg. "You said I'd like it, and I do!"

"I'm glad," he said.

"You said it'd make me forget about my dad, and I'm forgetting! I don't think I've stopped thinking about him since he got arrested. Only now I'm still thinking of him because I'm talking about him. But I don't mind talking about him." I turned to Johnny. "My dad's in jail," I explained. "He got arrested for child pornography. I don't think he did it, though. He's an artist, and sometimes he gets edgy with his art and doesn't realize things can be looked at the wrong way."

Johnny nodded. "You talk a lot."

"Do I?"

"Yeah, but that's okay. I like looking at you." He let his hand rest on my thigh.

I stared at the hand, trying to figure out what it was doing there. And then he took it away.

"How much did she take?" Johnny asked.

"A half. I'm giving her the other half right now."

Johnny pushed himself off the couch. "I'm going to see what's happening in the kitchen."

I lifted my chin and pouted. "Don't leave!"

He patted the top of my head. "I'll be back, sweetheart."

I giggled. The way he had patted me, like I was a dog. And then I thought of Po'Boy running around in the yard. That made me happy, and I smiled some more.

"Hey," Joey said. He grabbed my hand and put something in it. Another ecstasy pill. "I think you're ready."

Was I? I wanted to pop the pill in my mouth—anything to keep this feeling going strong—but a tiny, still-functioning part of my brain told me to hold off. "I have to go to the bathroom," I said. Which was true. But I also wanted to think.

He closed my fingers over the pill. "Take it in the bathroom," he said. "Don't tell anyone you have it. I already told them I didn't have any more."

People looked at me with knowing smiles as I stumbled toward the hallway. One guy lifted his water bottle like he was toasting me.

I got to the bathroom and closed the door. My reflection in the mirror gazed at me with hooded eyelids. My whole face sagged. My jaw ached, and I realized I'd been clenching my teeth. I looked like crap, but I felt so amazingly good. As much as I wanted to keep feeling this way, I knew I shouldn't take any more. I had to see Dad tomorrow, and my washed-up reflection told me I'd had enough.

I flushed the pill down the toilet.

When I came back to the living room, another guy was sitting on the couch with Joey. They moved apart, and I sank between them. Joey rubbed my thigh. "This is Tera," he said. "Tera, this is Mac."

"We met in the kitchen," Mac said, and only then did I recognize him. Sweat beaded on his shaved head.

I giggled. "Is that your real name?'

"Does it matter?" And then he leaned over and kissed me.

I wasn't sure what was happening at first. But then Joey's arm curled around my waist and slid up to fondle my breast. Joey kissed the back of my neck, and somehow I opened my mouth to Mac's kiss. Joey groaned behind me, his body pressing closer. Mac's fingers—I think they were Mac's fingers—massaged between my legs. *I don't care. It feels too good.* I moved closer to Mac. Joey moved closer to me. Was this happening? Should I stop it? It felt so good, I never wanted to stop.

I was vaguely aware of the pumping music, of people in the room, but I didn't care if they saw us. I didn't care about anything except how good it felt—and not because I was making out with two guys. *Two guys!* A part of my brain was in awe of myself. Where had this girl been hiding? But mostly I marveled at how my entire body radiated with pleasure—and not necessarily sexual pleasure, though that was part of it. More like the shuddering of an electric pulse vibrating my skin.

And then Mac pulled away. "This is getting too intense," he said. "I gotta do something."

"You want to fuck?" Joey said in my ear. I smiled and nodded. I did.

He took my hand, pulled me up from the couch. We walked down the hallway to the bedroom. Was that Mac following us? It was. He closed the door behind us. Joey took off his shirt. So did Mac.

"Wait," I said. "I didn't mean him, too."

"You serious?" Mac said.

"You heard her," Joey said. "Get out."

Mac put on his shirt and left. Before I could think more about it, Joey pulled me down on the bed. I ripped off my sweater and threw it in the corner. My bra was next. Joey unbuttoned his jeans.

And then I heard the door open. "Hey," a voice said. I looked over. Johnny was standing by the bed, staring down at me. "Can anybody join this party?"

"Um . . ." I looked to Joey. Joey would tell him to get out. But Joey was smiling at me. Did he not realize his uncle was standing there? I sat up on the bed and crossed my arms over my chest.

Johnny sat beside me. He tried to move my arms away, but I held them stiff. "Hey, now," he said. "Don't be like that."

Panic welled up in me. "I don't want to do this." I sounded like a little kid.

"It's okay," Joey said from my other side. "We can get under the blanket."

"You sure this is okay?" Johnny asked.

"Tera, come on." Joey touched my shoulder. "It's not a big deal. You were making out with that other guy."

I wanted to explain how making out with two guys was a long way from having sex with my boyfriend and his much older uncle, but I couldn't think clearly enough to form the words.

Joey leaned closer, like he was going to kiss me, but I shoved myself off the bed and darted to the corner where I'd thrown my bra and sweater. "Just leave me alone, okay? I want to get dressed."

Johnny sounded amused. "She wants us to leave her alone."

"No, she doesn't." Joey made a shooing motion with his hand. "Give us a minute."

Johnny left the room.

When we were alone, Joey came to the corner where I was sliding my arms through my bra straps. "Listen, Tera." He picked up my sweater before I could grab it. "We're just having fun."

And that's when I realized Joey must have planned this whole thing. That's why he left me alone earlier. So he could talk to his uncle and lay out how it would go.

I snatched my sweater. "It's not fun for me."

"It was fun ten minutes ago. Why not now?"

"Because." I could feel the drug wearing off, and I was starting to feel seriously disgusted with myself. I pulled my sweater over my head and made a beeline for the door. "I just don't want to, okay?"

Joey followed me to the living room. Heavy bass vibrated the floor, and a black light gave everything a ghostly glow.

I stood there and didn't know what to do. How was I going to get home? Mom would kill me if she had to come pick me up.

Joey backed me against the wall, his teeth glowing neon-white under the black light. "Stop running," he said. "You're embarrassing yourself."

I tried to move away. "I'm not running. I just want to go home."

He squeezed my breast. Not a caress. More like a honk. One hand tangled itself in my hair. The other snaked around my waist. His mouth felt wet on my ear. "I'm not taking you home yet. First I want to fuck. Just you and me."

"Stop it." I tried to pull away, but he wouldn't let go. No one seemed to notice. The woman with the talon fingernails leaned against the opposite wall, mesmerized by the lights on the stereo. The two people going at it on the recliner still had their heads under the blanket.

"Stop what? You don't like this?" His arms felt like tentacles wrapped around my waist. "I brought you here to fuck," he said. "So let's go *fuck*."

"Leave her alone, Joey."

Joey froze and eased his weight off me. We both looked toward the voice.

Sadie was sitting up on the recliner, glaring at him, her hair a tangled mess. Whoever she was making out with struggled to sit up, too. I recognized Sadie's friend, the one who'd picked her up from work the other night.

Joey's eyes wandered over each of us. Me, Sadie, Sadie's girlfriend. Then they fell on me again. He shook his head and stalked off toward the kitchen. "Fucking tease!" he announced to the ceiling. "A complete fucking bore!"

My cheeks flushed with humiliation. Tears stung my eyes. I blinked them dry before they could fall.

"Hey." Sadie got up from the recliner and put her hand on my arm. "You okay?"

I nodded, afraid of what would happen if I tried to talk.

"He's a prick. Ignore him."

I studied her face in the black light. Was she high, too? She didn't look it. A little drunk maybe.

"I know he likes you," she said.

I almost laughed, but instead my face crumpled and I had to cover it with my hands. *A fucking tease. A complete fucking bore.* Was he right? I felt like he might be right.

"You want to go somewhere and talk? Come on." She pulled me toward the screen door. I followed her like a lost sheep.

She guided me to the porch steps and pulled me down beside her. Her hand felt warm compared to the cold air.

"You can't just leave your girlfriend," I said.

"She's all right. She gets it."

We both sat looking out at the dark yard. Everyone else had gone inside. I pulled my knees in tight. My breath fogged in front of me.

"He's a complete dick," she said.

"That's not what you said before," I mumbled. "You said he was harmless."

"Did I?"

I nodded. I sounded bitchy and ungrateful. I knew I did.

"Sorry. I thought he *was* harmless." She shook her head. "He was with me, anyway."

"You dated him?" The thought didn't hurt, but it did surprise me.

"I wouldn't call it dating. We had sex."

"Oh." I waited for the flash of jealousy. It didn't come.

"He's not all that," she said. "He's not even that good."

"You don't think so?" And here I'd thought it was just me. My inexperience.

"And he's been lying to you about how old he is."

"What?" I whirled to face her. "How old is he?"

"I think he's twenty-two. Maybe twenty-three."

So much for his fake ID. Now I felt betrayed on top of everything else. "What an asshole!"

"Uh-huh."

I stared out at the yard, remembering what I'd let him do to me—not just Joey, but Mac and Johnny, too. And Joey had wanted it to happen.

Was he so starved for sex that he had to lie about his age to get me to sleep with him? He had probably lied about saving money for an apartment, too. And then he pretty much drugged me to get me to have a threesome . . . with his *uncle.* Maybe his mom wasn't even in prison. I could see him making up the whole prison story just to give himself a bad-boy image.

So he's some kind of bad boy? That's what Mr. Stewart had said when I showed him my Joey sketches. I'd gotten mad because it made me feel stupid. But he was right.

Shit. My *Girl on a Bus* painting. It probably sucked, too. I knew it did. I'd known it all along.

"You okay?" Sadie asked.

I closed my eyes. "Just pissed." It felt good to be pissed.

"Pissed at me?"

"Not at you."

"Do you need anything?"

No, I started to say. But then I thought of something she could do, something a friend would do for a friend.

"Do you think you could give me a ride home?"

CHAPTER 25

The county jail website made a big deal about what not to wear to a jail visit. No shorts or miniskirts. No tank tops. No hats. I put on an old sweatshirt and my loosest pair of jeans, told my mom I was going to work, and caught the bus downtown.

Fear sat in my gut like an ice block. I hadn't talked to my dad for more than two weeks, and I had no idea what he'd be like, how he'd act. I wanted him to know I was doing everything I could to help him. I wanted him to appreciate what I'd already given up.

And most of all, I wanted to hear what he had to say about the photos on his computer. I needed him to tell me they'd gotten there by accident.

The bus dropped me off right in front of the jailhouse. A woman and her little boy got off with me. All of us trudged up the short flight of steps. I opened the door for them, but the boy plunked himself down in front of the building's sand-filled ashtray. His mom pleaded with him to get up, but he kept wailing about how he didn't want to go in, how he didn't want to see his daddy. I almost knew how he felt. If I'd thought Dad was guilty, I'd have wanted to do the same thing.

I could still hear the kid crying as I walked to the front desk. A gray-haired woman checked my license against the approved visitors' list.

"I've never been here before," I said. "I'm not sure how this works."

"You'll get the hang of it."

I didn't want to get the hang of it. I wanted Dad out of here. I wanted to know he was innocent.

She pointed to a roped-off queue, where a couple of guards watched me approach with bored expressions. They made me put my purse in a locker. I went through a metal detector and got patted down. Then another guard walked me through a maze of corridors, where metal doors clanged shut behind me. Every door was guarded.

Finally, I got to the visitors' lobby, a big rectangle of cinder-block wall. It smelled like floor cleaner. Chairs were lined up on one side of a glass barrier, separated from each other by cubicle walls.

A guard led me to an empty chair and pointed to a telephone hanging on the divider wall. "You talk through that."

"Do you know when—?"

"Now you wait."

I clamped my mouth shut and waited. In the cubicle next to me, a woman sobbed.

Minutes passed. I breathed onto my cupped hands to warm them and rocked in my chair to keep the jitters at bay. The concrete walls were gray and bare except for a few signs posting the rules for visits. Two guards hovered in the corners.

The woman next to me finished her visit. Another woman took her place. This one kept tapping her foot and sniffling. I imagined she was like me: tense and freezing and trying not to think about what this person she loved was doing here. I looked around for the woman with the little boy but didn't see her. Maybe the little boy didn't have to see his daddy after all.

My eyes were starting to burn from staring at the empty space on the other side of the glass. I closed them, just for a second, and when I opened them, there he was. A guard was bringing him in.

I almost didn't recognize him. He kept his head down, but I saw how his face sagged. His eyes were red and puffy. His orange prison jumpsuit hung on him, and he shuffled when he walked. The guard practically pushed him into the chair behind the glass.

I fumbled for the phone and pressed it to my ear. "Dad!"

No response. He looked at his hands, rubbed the ink stains on his fingers.

"Dad." I waved my hand at the glass. "Pick up the phone."

His eyes flicked toward the movement. I watched him take a deep breath, watched him stare at his lap before picking up the phone. *Come on, Dad. Look at me.* Slowly, he lifted his eyes to mine.

"Tera." His voice sounded tinny and distant. I almost cried when he spoke my name.

I searched for something to say. All my planning, and I didn't know what to say. "You look good," I began.

He grunted. "You didn't have to do this."

"Visit you? I wanted to." I made myself smile even though my heart was breaking to see him like this.

He waved a hand. Impatient. "The money for art school. You spent it. Why did you do that?"

My smile wavered. "To help you."

"I didn't ask for your help."

My chest tightened. This wasn't right. He was supposed to be grateful. "Dad . . ."

"Do you know what I went through to save all that money?"

"I had to get you a lawyer. Someone who knows what they're doing."

"Oh, yeah." Sarcasm dripped from his tone. "Charlotte Gross definitely knows what she's doing. She must be an expert at finding naïve girls and taking their money."

I shook my head. "It wasn't like that." Was it? Did she swindle me? Or was Dad saying all this because he knew how guilty he was?

"It doesn't matter. You blew it, Tera."

How could he say that? After what I did for him. "She'll help you."

"You *had* to spend that money, didn't you? And now you're stuck here. Stuck here so you can turn out just like your mom."

"I'm not stuck. I'll save up so I can go next year."

He pinched the bridge of his nose, like talking to me was giving him a headache. "All the work I put into you. All that time I spent molding you so you could study with the best, so you wouldn't have to struggle like I struggled."

How to make him understand? "The lawyer will get you out of here. To me, that's more important than—"

His hand cut the air. "It's *not* more important. Nothing is more important than you. Goddammit, Tera. How could you be so stupid?"

I shrank back like he'd slapped me.

"You can't help me," he said. "*She* can't help me."

"Why not?" *Please don't tell me you did it.* "Why can't she help you?"

"I'm sick of all this pussyfooting around. Didn't she tell you what they found?"

Please, no. "You didn't mean to." I shook my head. "You're innocent."

When he laughed, I wanted to bury my head and cover my ears. "You think anyone will believe that?" he sneered.

"She's good," I said, desperate now for him to agree with me. "She's won a bunch of cases and she'll prove that—"

"I'm tired of hiding. You don't know what it's like to spend your whole life hiding."

"Stop it, Dad." If I kept shaking my head, it wouldn't be true.

"Do I have to draw you a picture?" *THWACK!* His palm struck the glass.

I flinched, eyes wide.

"You're not hearing me!"

But I *was* hearing him. Guilty. My dad was guilty.

The guard behind him growled something and pointed at the glass. Dad murmured a reply and the guard stepped back.

"So now you know," Dad said.

My throat swelled. I closed my eyes and lowered my head. All those kids being forced to undress, to pose. All those scared kids. Their lives torn up so men like my dad could jerk themselves off.

The fear in my stomach, the built-up anxiety, the disgust. All of it melted into black bile and snaked its way toward my throat.

"Does your mom know you blew your future?"

His tinny voice in my ear made me shudder. I leaned forward, holding my stomach. "She knows."

"Listen, Tera. You can still go to art school. Get a deferment on your scholarship. Then let me help you—"

"I don't want your help."

He choked out a laugh. "You *need* my help. I was the sculptor and you were the clay, whether you like it or not. You wouldn't be the artist you are without me."

I glared at him through tears that froze in my eyes. "You didn't make me," I said. I had to say it to make it true. I wanted no part of his sick world.

"Jesus Christ, Tera, what do you think—"

SLAM! I hung up on him. His mouth kept moving, but I didn't have to hear it.

He jabbed his finger at my phone, then at me. *Pick up the goddamn phone!*

I stood up, waved my arm at the guard. Dad changed tactics, put on his pleading face. I tried not to look, but I could read his lips. *I'm sorry. Tera. Don't go. I'm sorry.*

I watched him mouth those empty, silent words, watched his desperation. Then I turned my back and made my escape. Through the clang of metal doors and the cold maze of corridors. Past the guards with their guns and bleak expressions. Into the drizzling rain. The rain felt good on my skin. Clean.

I ran to the bus stop, not bothering to open my umbrella. On the bus, I punched in the number for Charlotte Gross. She didn't pick up, but I was happy to leave her a message. There wouldn't be any more money, I told her. When the retainer ran out, that was it. I was done.

CHAPTER 26

Cuckoo Bird

Her dad sat on the edge of her bed, her sketchbook in his lap.

"It's at the back," she said, and watched him flip the thick pages. When he turned to the right one, he didn't say anything. She didn't look at the drawing. Instead, she watched his eyes move over the page. Maybe he'd burn it like her mom had burned the drawing of Haley in her Titanic *pose.*

"You're getting better," he said. "Not bad for a nine-year-old." His big finger waved over the dark smudges shadowing the girl. Tera didn't want to look at what she'd done. She wanted to turn her face to the wall, just like the naked girl in the picture.

"Too much gray, though. See?" He pointed to a corner of the drawing. "This is where the light was coming from, so your shadows are too heavy."

"Okay," she said.

"Let me see the photo and I'll show you."

She didn't move.

"Where's the photo, Tera?"

Her throat closed up, making it hard to talk. "I don't have it."

"What happened to it?"

"I threw it away."

Silence. Then a big sigh. "Why would you do that?"

She swallowed, trying to think of an answer he would like. Because looking at it made her feel scared. Because what she saw in the picture made her want to hide where no one could find her.

Those answers were no good, though. He'd get mad, call her a baby. He wouldn't want to look at her anymore.

Then she had it. "I didn't want Mom to find it."

That made him smile. "Good thinking. But listen." He closed the sketchbook and turned to look at her. "Are you listening?"

"Yes."

"We have to take another picture."

A bolt of fear stabbed into her back, made her sit up stiff like she'd been electrocuted. "I don't want to."

He touched her cheek with the back of his fingers. "Don't you want to get better?"

"Yes."

"Then you need to practice."

It was hard to get the words out, so she shook her head.

His mouth twitched, and he wiped at a smear of paint on his hands. She thought he might smile and say it was okay, but then he blew out his breath, and she knew he was fed up with her.

She bit her lip and didn't look at his face. He'd yell. She knew it was coming, but the sound cutting the silence made her jump.

"Why do you have to make everything so hard? You think I like wasting my time trying to make something of you? You want to be like your mom when you grow up? You want to be a fucking cuckoo-bird housewife?"

"No." She tried to swallow a big block in her throat, but it wouldn't go down. She almost made a crying sound, but she managed to choke it back by holding her breath.

"You're more like her every day. I get so sick of both of you."

He got up to leave and didn't hear her say she was sorry. Maybe she hadn't said it. She tried again.

"I'm sorry."

He turned before he got to the door. She pulled her shoulders in close and stared at her feet.

"You want me to leave, Tera? You want me to leave forever?"

She shook her head.

"I don't want to have to leave, but I can't stay here if I have to fight the both of you."

"You don't have to fight me."

He came back and sat on top of her sketchpad. It bent under his weight.

"It'll be easy," he said. "I'll help you."

He tugged at the front of her shirt, but she glued her arms to her side and didn't move.

"Stop fighting me, Tera."

She loosened her arms for just a second, and with one hard yank, he pulled her shirt over her head. The cool air raised goose bumps on her skin. She crossed her arms over her chest and hunched herself together.

"That's better," he whispered, his breath damp in her ear. One hand snaked around her, tugging at her stiff arms. His other hand moved the hair away from her neck.

She tried not to move, but the tears came anyway, slipping down her face and making her jaw quiver.

He didn't notice. He wasn't looking at her face, too busy trying to get her arms away from her chest. She locked her elbows, but he was strong. He pressed her against the mattress, saying, "Hold still," and peeled her arms back, one by one.

At first she didn't recognize the sound that came out of her. It started in her throat, low and quiet. Then it got too heavy to hold inside, and out it came, growing louder and louder. Just one cry that stretched her throat and made her mouth hinge open like it'd never close. She tried to stop, but maybe two brains were inside her. One controlling and the other watching. The cuckoo bird and the girl.

He let go of her and sprang back, blinking like he'd got woken up from a dream. She heard him say her name, heard him plead, "Sorry, I'm sorry," but the sound inside her kept going. Maybe it was the cuckoo bird making all that noise. The cuckoo bird didn't want to stop. Not until he went away and it was safe to take a breath.

CHAPTER 27

Mr. Stewart always said that art, in whatever form it takes, is a kind of therapy for creative people. Songwriters compose songs. Poets write poetry. Musicians play music. He had said my best artwork was a reflection of things that happened in my personal life. A girl crying because her dog ran away, or celebrating her birthday with her parents, or sitting on a bus dreaming about her boyfriend. Sometimes the girl was blonde, sometimes brunette. Sometimes she was a child, other times a grown woman. Sometimes she took the form of an animal. It didn't matter. She was always me.

Mom's car was gone when I got home from the jail. The house was silent and still. I took my sketchpad to the kitchen table and thought about what Mr. Stewart said—how art was therapy.

And then I didn't allow myself to think. I started sketching, first the outline of a bed, a window, a desk. After a few minutes, I looked down at what I'd drawn. It was my room as it always looked, the room where I slept and dreamed. The room where Dad had taken that picture.

I sketched in a body on the bed, drew an oval shape for the head. Just like my dad had taught me. I imagined crosshairs on the oval, invisible markers for the eyes, nose, and mouth. But when it came time to draw the face, my hand froze.

What did Dad do, alone in his studio, after Mom and I went to bed?

I pictured him as a troll in the darkness, hunched over his computer screen, stroking himself while he grunted and drooled.

I looked down at my oval, empty and waiting for a face. Mr. Stewart's stupid slogan kept haunting me. *Find your muse.*

My cheeks hardened like stone, all the muscles stiff. I clenched my jaw and sketched a face into the oval, but the features came out melted and jumbled, like Salvador Dalí's clocks or Picasso's *Guernica*. The whole thing looked wrong.

And just like that, the rock that was my real face melted in a lava flow of shame and anger. I could barely see when I gripped my pencil like a dagger and jabbed it at the paper. Over and over, until the face became a scar, torn and jagged and clotted with rash.

• • •

Joey and I worked the same shift the next day. I didn't want to face him, not after what he did to me, and not after what he called me. Would he apologize? More likely, he'd ignore me. I told myself that if things got too awkward, I could quit and find another job, maybe one that paid better tips. Now that I didn't have to pay Dad's lawyer, I could concentrate on saving for art school.

Joey sat smoking in the break room, his chair tilted back on two legs. "Hey," he said. Like nothing at all was wrong.

I walked past him to the row of lockers, my body a taut bowstring. I felt his eyes imprinted on my back as I shoved my key into the lock. It opened with a snap.

"So you're ignoring me?" His voice like a scratch down my neck.

I stuffed my purse into my locker.

"Whatever," he said.

I whirled to face him. "Don't act like nothing's wrong."

He blinked at me. "What did I do? You're the one who left the party."

"I left because of you. You're going to pretend you don't remember?"

"I don't!" He gave me that sly half-grin that had had me swooning a few days ago. "I was pretty wasted."

I could hear Cam and Mr. Barnes talking in the hallway, which meant they could hear us, too. Now wasn't the time to bring up the fact that I'd almost had a threesome with Joey and his uncle, that Joey had drugged me up and brought me there just for that purpose.

Still, I had to stand up for myself. "You called me a *fucking bore*," I said.

I watched my words soak in and pry up the supposedly sunken memory. He rubbed the back of his neck. "I really said that?"

"Yeah, you did. And a lot more, but I don't want to talk about it."

"Then I'm sorry. Really, I am." He reached for me. "Do you forgive me?"

I waved his hand away. Why had I ever thought he'd be good for me? "You're such a liar," I said. "You're not sorry at all."

"I *am* sorry." He looked down at his hands. "I think you're really cool. You're edgy, you know? So I thought . . . It doesn't matter what I thought. Obviously, I was wrong."

Since when did I give off an edgy vibe? I slammed my locker shut.

He kept talking. "You don't even realize how great you are. No one as smart as you would ever go out with me. And you're an artist. I haven't told you how cool I think that is."

The padlock clunked as I fumbled to close it. I wasn't buying it, but I still turned my head to steal a glance at his face—just in case he looked sincere. He had his head down, scrolling through something on his phone. He didn't see me looking. His mouth was still going.

"Seriously, Tera. I'm really sorry. Sometimes when I get wasted, I lose control."

"Maybe that should tell you something."

"And you're more to me than . . . ." He pushed a button on his phone and shoved it into his back pocket. "Than just a fuck."

"That's beautiful, Joey."

He got up from his chair and leaned against the lockers, his arm forming a scaffold over my head. I smelled pizza sauce, smoke in his hair, a mint disguising stale breath. "You have to believe me," he said. "I didn't mean to hurt you."

Just like Dad.

"You're so full of it," I said.

He stared at me, a cat sizing up its prey. I ducked under his arm and headed for the door.

"Be that way!" he called after me. "Be a fucking bitch!"

I kept walking, pretending his words didn't hurt. I passed Cam and Mr. Barnes. They were quiet, both of them studying their shoes. They must have heard every word.

I tried to concentrate on work after that, but I kept forgetting things. Extra napkins, silverware, refills on drinks. I got stiffed more than once.

And just as suddenly as it had started, the dinner rush died. While Cam restocked the prep table, Joey volunteered to help clean the dining room. I couldn't help watching him as he tossed dirty plates and forks into a bin. I cringed when I thought about how I had sketched him. How I had lay in bed and fantasized about him. How I had let him grope me and pant on me and use me.

He worked fast, his bin overflowing with dirty dishes. And then I saw him pick up something else from a table—something that wasn't a dish—and shove it into the pocket of his jeans. He paused to stretch his back, his eyes drifting back and forth. Then he whipped out his phone. He read the screen. His body got very still.

Sadie came up behind me. "Good to look at," she said. "Not so good to touch."

I smiled, distracted.

She popped a piece of ice in her mouth. "He does have a nice ass, though."

"Too bad his personality doesn't match."

"He looks pissed," Sadie said. "I'd stay away."

Not pissed. Scared. I studied him from behind the server station. He had his phone in an iron grip and was staring at the screen with a slack-jawed expression. Like how my dad had looked when the cop handed him the search warrant. Huh.

My shift ended at five o'clock. I was in the break room, getting my stuff out of my locker, when Sadie's voice drifted from the hallway. "What the hell, Joey? I told you no."

A second later, she burst into the break room. She pulled a cigarette from her apron and lit it with one angry flick of her lighter.

"What happened?" I asked.

She sucked in smoke before answering. "The prick's trying to borrow money from me. Like I have extra money to throw away on his drug problem."

"Joey?"

"Who else?" Smoke gusted out of her mouth. "Shoot me in the face if I ever again try to give you guy advice."

I thought about Joey taking something off the table and putting it in his pocket. That was Sadie's table. If Joey was stealing tips, I should tell someone. But what if it was a book of matches? Or a lighter? It could have been anything.

"How were your tips today?" I asked. "I got stiffed a few times."

She shrugged, crushed out her cigarette. "Okay, I guess. I have to get back. You taking the bus home?"

"Yeah."

"If you want to wait, I'll give you a ride."

"That's okay." I didn't want to be around Joey any longer than necessary. "Thanks, anyway."

As I walked down the hallway, I caught Joey watching me. He scowled. My first instinct was to look away, but I made myself hold his gaze.

"What are you looking at?" he sneered.

"Nothing much," I said. "Have a good day."

• • •

When I got home from work, Mom was on the couch—not lying down, but sitting. Without the TV on. She had a gardening magazine in her lap. Was she actually reading? The magazine looked brand new.

"How was work?" she asked.

"Fine."

She closed her magazine. "Are you okay? Did something happen?"

I wanted to tell someone, but there was no way I was going to share with her what happened between Joey and me. "No," I said. "I'm just tired."

"You want me to fix you something to eat?"

"I ate at work."

"Oh." She bit her lip. I knew she was trying.

"But thanks anyway," I said.

The phone rang from the end table by the couch. Both of us jumped. Mom stared at the caller ID, but I was too far away to see it.

"Who is it?" I asked.

"No one."

It rang a few more times and then stopped.

"Was it the lawyer?" I asked.

She shook her head. "A bill collector. Nothing you have to worry about."

Of course I didn't believe her.

Then it rang again. This time I picked it up. "Hello?"

A woman's automated voice came on. "This is Liberty Bell. You have a collect call from . . ." A pause, and then my dad saying his own name: "Tim Waters."

The sound of his voice made me panic. I almost dropped the phone before I hung up.

"Is it him?" Mom asked.

Then it started ringing again. Mom and I stared at each other. She didn't know I'd gone to visit him. She didn't know I wanted nothing to do with him. After the second ring, she reached for the phone. "Give me it," she said. "He can't keep calling here."

It rang again. She reached for the phone, but I moved away from her. I was the one who had to tell him not to call. I held the phone to my ear, pushed the Answer button. "Hello?"

The same automated message: "This is Liberty Bell. You have a collect call from . . ."

"Dad," said the voice.

"If you would like to accept this call, press zero now."

I pressed zero.

The line crackled. My dad cleared his throat. "Tera, it's me. Don't hang up."

I held my breath.

"I . . . I want you to know I'm sorry for . . . for what I said."

I stayed silent, waiting.

"I never meant to hurt you. You know that."

For years, I'd told myself that same thing. Because he'd stopped doing it. He'd stopped after I cried and kicked. So I made myself believe what he wanted me to believe: That he didn't know any better. That he had never meant to hurt me.

But he *did* know better. And he didn't care if he hurt me. As long as he got what he wanted.

"I don't want to talk to you," I said. "Don't call me again."

"But I ca—"

My thumb stabbed the Off button.

Mom stared into my face, her hand covering her mouth. "You know he's guilty, don't you?"

I nodded.

"His lawyer told you?"

I put down the phone before answering. "She told me they found photos on his computer. She said he could have downloaded them by accident. And then I went to see him, and he . . ." I rubbed my arms. "He didn't deny anything."

"Good." She let out her breath. "Then maybe he won't fight it."

But he *was* fighting it. I had paid for a lawyer so he could do just that.

"You should have told me what you found," I said.

"I told you I found something on his computer. I didn't know how else to say it. I didn't want you mixed up in it."

"But I *am* mixed up in it."

She pressed her knuckles to her chin. "I always told myself he'd leave you alone because he loves you so much."

"You knew what he was?" I squinted at her, my voice cracking. "How long did you know?"

"I swear to you. I only found the pictures on his computer a few days before the police came."

"And you didn't think anything was going on before that?"

"I didn't have proof. He was careful. And whenever I confronted him, he made it sound like *I* was the one being unreasonable."

I clenched my teeth. Yes, he was good at that.

"I kept going back and forth," she said. "Was I the crazy one, or was he? And you always stood up for him, so I figured he hadn't done anything to you. You were like hallowed ground to him. He always protected you."

I couldn't believe what she was telling me. "Mom." I waited for her to look me in the eye. "*You* should have protected me."

She slumped. Her hands covered her face.

Maybe I should have felt sorry for her, but she'd been such a shitty mother. It felt good to see her cry.

It felt good for only a second.

I put my arm around her shaking shoulders. "It's okay," I whispered, even though it wasn't. I kept saying it, though, and she kept nodding her head. Like if we agreed everything was okay—if we said it over and over—we'd make it come true.

CHAPTER 28

Comic-Book Hero

"Dad! Look at this!"

She had her phone out, ready to show him. A comment on Facebook from an art professor in California. He had called her a prodigy.

She slipped, almost stumbled down the stairs. Her new phone—a gift for her thirteenth birthday—slipped out of her hand. It bounced down the basement stairs. Breathing hard, she held the railing with one hand and picked her way down. Her phone lay in pieces at the bottom of the stairs. She'd had it for less than two months. Dad said if she lost or broke it, not to bother asking for a new one.

"Tera, is that you?"

"Yeah, it's me." She scooped up the pieces of her phone and shoved them in her pocket. Maybe she could fix it before he found out.

"Hold on a second," he called. "I'll be right out."

She heard him moving around in the little room at the back of his studio. His archive room. He didn't like her going in there, so she wandered over to his desk. On top was a pile of pen-and-ink drawings that looked like all his other stuff: lizard people and dog people and heroes with big muscles. Then something else caught her eye. She pulled it from the stack and stared.

It was her—a comic-book version of her as a little girl, maybe eight or nine years old. A big bald man with clenched fists came at her from the opposite side of the page. In the first panel, she glared at him with narrowed eyes. And in the next, she aimed a karate kick at the bad guy's face. The thought bubble floating near the man's head said, Shit . . . I got more than I bargained for.

"What are you doing?"

She jumped. She hadn't heard his footsteps. "Nothing."

"Snooping?" Her dad plucked the drawing from her hand.

"Just seeing what you're working on."

"And what do you think?"

She shrugged. "It's cool."

"But?"

"I don't know karate."

He rolled his eyes. "It's not supposed to be real life."

"You're making me into a comic book?" she asked.

"It's a graphic novel, not a comic book . . . And no. Sorry to disappoint you. No one would buy a graphic novel about a little girl beating up bad guys."

"Oh."

"So what'd you want to show me?" he asked.

She could still tell him about the art professor's comment on Facebook without showing him on her phone. But being called a prodigy didn't seem as exciting as it had a few minutes ago. Now she was thinking of something she'd been trying to forget for a long time. The problem was, she couldn't forget it till she knew for sure it was gone.

So it was best just to ask, while they were kind of on the topic.

"You don't have that photo of me anymore. Do you?"

He sucked air through his nose, the sound he made when she was getting on his nerves. "What do you think?"

She shrugged.

"You got rid of it yourself," he said.

"But it was on your computer."

He squinted at her. "What makes you say that?"

"It had to be on your computer if you made a print of it."

"God, Tera. That was so long ago. I only did it to help you get better. You know that, right?"

"I know."

"So why dredge it up? Is it because of this?" He held up the drawing of her doing the karate kick. "I can't draw my own daughter?"

"You can draw me."

"Then why are you acting like this? Jesus Christ, you always—"

"But don't draw me like that."

He blinked like she'd flicked him in the face. "Like what? You don't like being a hero?"

"It's not that."

"You have something against karate? It's not karate, by the way. It's tae kwon do."

She hesitated, not sure what it was about the drawing that made her nervous. He'd never sketched her before as far as she knew, so why was she freaking out now?

"Don't turn into your mother, Tera. I have high hopes for you."

And then it came to her. She knew why she wanted to tear the drawing into little pieces.

"Did you hear what I said?" he asked.

"Yes."

"Then tell me what I said."

"You said, 'Don't turn into your mother.'"

"Glad to see you're listening. Now go back upstairs. I need to get some work done."

But she needed him to understand, and it seemed important enough to risk making him mad. "And did you hear what I said?" she asked.

"No, I must've missed that." He looked amused. "What did you say?"

"I said, 'Don't draw me like that.' Draw me the age I am now, but not like that."

His face changed, his smile blowing away like a balloon with a rip in it. "And what do you find that's so wrong with it?"

"I don't like it," she told him. "I don't like being a little girl."

CHAPTER 29

Monday in Art class, Mr. Stewart had us working with clay. He encouraged us to get to know the clay by squeezing it, pinching it, tearing it apart. Most kids were making cups or bowls, but I wanted to get Mr. Stewart's attention, so instead of a bowl, I decided to sculpt a dog.

Mr. Stewart walked the aisles between our tables, smiling and encouraging, giving pointers. But when he got to me, he didn't stop. I was supposed to be his favorite student, and he didn't stop.

The clay was cool to the touch, pliable and soft. Just like me in my dad's hands. Dad had said it perfectly. He was the sculptor, and I was the clay. All those years he spent mixing and shaping and chipping away at me. Until finally I turned out exactly how he wanted. His little sheep. His loyal dog. His blind follower. No wonder he got pissed when I gave up the art institute to help him. I was his lifetime achievement, his sickening work of art.

I shaped the clay to form the dog's legs, my hands like clumsy paddles. Mr. Stewart reached the end of the aisle and turned back. His eyes fell on me, darted away. One of my dog's legs broke off and plopped to my desk. This was pointless. I closed my hand around my clay dog and squeezed it in my fist until the sculpture became a shapeless mass. *Tabula rasa.*

That's what I wanted to be. A blank slate.

After class, I stayed sitting at my desk. Mr. Stewart had his nose buried in his grade book, pretending not to notice me. When the room emptied out, I scraped my chair against the floor.

He glanced up from his papers, his glasses slipping down his nose. "You need something, Tera?"

There was so much I wanted to say, but I didn't know where to start. "If you're not too busy."

"No, I guess not." He stood and came to my desk, his eyes scoping the hallway. He stopped a foot from my desk. "What is it?"

Where to start? "I entered something for the contest."

"That's great. Can I see it?"

"I uploaded it to their website. Anybody can see it. But I don't think it's good enough to win."

"I'll take a look. It might be better than you think. And you still have time to enter another painting. The deadline's tomorrow, right? You could work on something tonight, or you could—"

"They're not extending my scholarship," I said.

He took a moment to process that. "Oh."

"So even if I win the contest, I don't know if I'll be able to go."

"You can apply for the scholarship again. You know that, right? They award two every year." When I didn't say anything, he peered at my face. "Something else happened, didn't it?"

I focused on the bits of clay scattered on my desk. "I know he's guilty," I said.

"I'm sorry, Tera."

I shrugged, like it didn't matter, like I hadn't given up the only future I had ever wanted in order to help him.

"You can't let this stop you from going to art school," he said.

I thought of the face I'd drawn with its clotted rash. "I tried to draw the other day, and . . ." I shook my head.

"Trying is good, even if it didn't turn out well."

He didn't understand. "It didn't feel right at all. It felt . . ." I picked at the clay buried under my fingernails. "Dirty somehow, like I was scraping out muck."

"Because of what I told you? About digging out the pain? If that's the case, I take it back."

"I don't know. I don't think so."

"Then, what? Talk to me, Tera."

He'd been ignoring me for days, and now he wanted to talk? "You won't even look at me in class," I said. "Did I do something? Are you afraid my dad's sleaziness might rub off?"

"Of course not. I . . ." He bit back whatever else he was going to say.

"Never mind," I said and got up to leave.

"Tera, stay. I need to tell you something."

"What?"

"I was ignoring you, I admit. But not because I wanted to."

"So . . . someone put a gun to your head?"

"Just listen to me. I'm trying to explain. I had a dictate from my boss. Principal Meyer told me to back off from you. He said it didn't look right."

"What does that even mean?"

"Because your dad got arrested for child pornography and he didn't want anyone to think I might somehow be . . ." He heaved in a breath. "Comforting you in an inappropriate manner."

Shame slithered around my neck like a snake. I thought of Mac and Joey and Johnny. What I'd done with them. What I'd let them do to me. "Because if my dad collects child pornography," I said, "I must be some kind of slut."

"I didn't say that."

"And you're not allowed to talk to sluts. You're not allowed to look at them either."

"Stop saying that. You're degrading yourself by saying that."

"And yet you're talking to me now. Aren't you afraid someone will see?"

"I'm allowed to talk to you."

"But you can't get too close. Is that what Principal Meyer said?"

His mouth twitched. "I can't show an interest."

"Oh." I pressed my lips together, nodded. My warped reflection glinted off his glasses. Two tiny splats of me.

"I'm sorry." He moved his head and my mirror images winked out. "I'm sorry for all this misunderstanding."

Of course he was sorry. So was Joey. So was my dad.

"You're okay?" he asked me.

I made myself shrug. Like it didn't matter. Like it didn't hurt at all.

• • •

As I walked down the hallway, a self-portrait formed in my head. I knew exactly how hurt and anger looked. My face long and pale. Blank eyes. A slash for a mouth. All my features blaring in stark light.

Once outside, the sun beat down on me, hardening my anger like an oven bakes clay. The bus sat shuddering by the curb. I was about to board, but a hand on my arm held me back.

"Tera, wait." It was Haley, her eyes wide and blinking.

"I can't talk," I said. "I'll miss the bus."

"But I met with that lawyer guy. Herman Liebowitz." She studied my face. "Did he call you?"

The bus released its brakes in an ear-splitting hiss. "No," I said. "Not since last week."

"Oh." She looked confused. "He was supposed to call you."

"Well, he didn't."

The bus engine roared to life. The door rattled shut. "Wait!" I knocked on the glass, but the huge tires were already inching away from the curb. My arm dropped to my side. Shit.

Haley dangled the keys to her mom's Audi. "I can give you a ride."

"I don't want a ride," I snapped. "I want to know why I had to miss the bus. What did you tell the lawyer?" I knew Dad was guilty, but I still didn't think he had done anything to Haley. He always avoided her, called her a snotty little bitch. And he knew she was a huge blabbermouth. "Did you lie to him? What did you tell him?"

Haley's face paled. She shook her head. "I don't want to talk about it."

Of course she didn't. I had missed the bus so she could have her moment of drama. Sweat trickled down my neck. "Why are you doing this, Haley?"

"Huh?" That innocent blink again.

"Is it so everyone can see how nice you are to talk to someone like me?"

Her eyes narrowed. "Why are you being such a bitch? All I wanted was to help you."

We were starting to draw an audience, but I didn't care. I was sick of her phony sweetness, sick of everyone adoring her because she was pretty and drove a nice car and had normal parents.

"Did my dad actually do something to you, Haley? I'm sure everyone wants to hear so they can feel sorry for you."

"Stop it. I'm trying to help you."

"Trying to help by making sure the entire school knows? I saw what you posted on the school forum. 'Don't study at Tera's house because her dad's a child molester.'" My laugh sounded hollow. "Ever since we were kids, you've pretended to help me, but all you really want is to stab me in the back."

The whole time I was spouting off, she just stared at me like I was crazy. Like she felt sorry for me.

Her boyfriend Sam peeled away from the stunned circle of kids who had stopped to listen. He put his hand on Haley's shoulder, murmured in her ear. "Let's go."

That seemed to shake her. She let him lead her away.

And then she stopped and turned back, her face crumbling. "You have no idea what you're talking about," she told me. She was crying. Real tears. "Honestly, you have no idea."

CHAPTER 30

When I got home from school, Herman Liebowitz called the house. I knew who it was from the caller ID.

Mom answered it from her bedroom before I could grab it in the kitchen. She was already talking when I lifted it to my ear.

"She's not here," Mom was saying. "And please stop calling. If she wanted to talk to you, she'd call you. She has your number."

A pause. "You are aware, Ms. Waters, that I can have your daughter subpoenaed? I'd rather not do that, so if I could please just talk to her."

"I'm here," I said into the phone. "Mom, it's okay. You can hang up."

"I'm not hanging up."

"Am I speaking to Tera Waters?" the lawyer said.

I liked how composed he sounded even with Mom barking at him. "Yes," I said. "I'm Tera."

"I'm wondering if you can come to my office tomorrow morning to speak with me. I have something I'd like to show you, before your father's trial gets under way."

"Is this about Haley Sweeney? About what she told you?"

"Who?" I heard papers shuffling. "No, it's nothing to do with her. Will you come?"

Mom breathed into the phone.

"What time?" I asked.

"You can come before school, I'll be here. Say seven o'clock?"

"That's fine. Let me get your address."

I scribbled down his directions and told him I'd see him in the morning.

Mom came into the kitchen. "At least let me go with you."

"Do you know what it's about?"

Mom crossed her arms over her chest. "He probably wants you to testify."

"He said he had something to show me."

"I don't know anything about that. Will you let me go with you? In case you need me?"

I studied her face. The way her eyes pleaded. "Yeah, okay," I said. I couldn't imagine what she could do for me, but I'd let her play at being a good mom. She definitely needed the practice.

• • •

And still my day wasn't over. I had to work that evening. With Joey. I dreaded having to see him, deal with him.

The first hour of work passed slowly. Joey hadn't clocked in yet. I filled the salad bar and stood around the server station, waiting for customers. No tables came in, but the phone kept ringing for carryout orders.

After I keyed in yet another carryout order, I wandered back to the prep table to see if Cam needed help. He'd already seen the order and was smearing sauce onto a circle of dough. He dropped the ladle into the tub and picked up a handful of cheese with his gloved hand.

"You need any help?" I asked. "It's dead out there."

He smiled. "Do you think you could scratch my ear?"

"Sure."

And that's what I was doing when Joey came past—scratching Cam's ear.

Joey stopped in his tracks. A mean little smile curled his lips. "Scratching an itch, Tera?" He made a jerking-off motion with his hand. "Keep practicing. You're not that good at it."

A flush crept up my neck. I suddenly felt very small.

Joey kept walking. Cam followed him with his eyes. "What the hell? What was that about?"

It was about me not wanting to have a threesome at his uncle's party. A *fucking tease*, he had called me. But I couldn't explain that to Cam. "I have no idea," I said.

Sadie clocked in a few minutes later. "How're you doing?" she asked me. "Is Joey being an asshole?"

I shrugged.

"Because if he's being an asshole, I'll kick his ass."

We started to get busy then. A bunch of tables came in at the same time, and I was hurrying so much that I made a mistake typing in an order. I didn't notice the mistake on the ticket until after I'd brought out their drinks. By then the pizza was made and ready for the oven.

And of course it was Joey, not Cam, who'd made the order. Cam smiled at me as he scooped up a handful of pepperoni. I tried to smile back.

"Hey, Joey?" I said.

Joey's eyes shifted to me.

"That pizza with the green pepper is actually supposed to be mushroom."

Joey used the sauce ladle to point to the monitor above his head. "It says green pepper."

"I know. I'm sorry. I messed up."

He tossed the ladle back into the sauce tub. "Maybe you should spend more time doing your job and less time stalking me."

"I'm not stalking you."

Cam kept laying down pieces of pepperoni like the job required every bit of his concentration.

"You think I haven't noticed the way you follow me around?" Joey tilted the botched pizza into the garbage. "I hate to break it to you, but I sampled your goods, and I'm not paying."

My ears burned. I wanted to walk away and hide my face, but I made myself stand there and look at him as though he hadn't just cut me in half. It was one thing to let my dad manipulate me, but I was done letting this jerk-off make me feel bad about myself. I did enough of that on my own.

I was trying to think of something to say—something that would show him he couldn't hurt me—when Mr. Barnes hurried past with a tub of dirty dishes. "Tera, I just sat two tables in your section. You need to move it along."

"Okay," I said. I knew I should stay and finish this, but I was glad for an excuse to leave. "Be right there."

Joey laughed. "Hey, Tera. Two at the same time—just like the other night."

I whirled on him. "Stop it! What did I ever do to you?"

Joey pretended not to hear me. He leaned closer to Cam. "You should have seen her the other night, going at it, with me *and* this other guy. *At the same time.* I can't remember the guy's name." He looked over at me, his lips curled up in a smug little smile. I was losing this battle, and he knew it. "Did you catch his name, Tera, before you started taking your clothes off for him?"

"You're such a complete and total dick! Why don't you tell Cam what really happened?"

Cam grabbed a fistful of mushrooms. "I don't think I should be hearing this."

"You definitely need to hear this," Joey said. "You first, Tera." The way he lounged against the table, the way he talked down to Cam and me—even the way he smirked—reminded me so much of my dad.

"He's pissed," I said, "because I wouldn't have sex with him and his sleazy uncle."

Cam dropped a pile of mushrooms on his pizza.

"But tell him the whole thing," Joey said, folding his arms over his chest. "I thought she liked older men. I thought for sure she'd taken her clothes off for her dad."

"You're such an asshole." I wanted to hit him, scratch his eyes out. Instead I clenched my pen inside my apron pocket. I clenched it so hard that my fingers hurt. "Just stop talking."

He looked amused, holding up his hands in a helpless gesture. "What am I doing?"

"You know exactly what you're doing! Trying to pretend I'm some kind of slut because of what my dad did." I couldn't hold back my anger any longer, and I hurled my pen at him. It bounced off his apron and fell to the floor. "What my dad did has *nothing* to do with who I am!"

Mr. Barnes came rushing toward us, his face tight with anger. "What are you guys *doing* back here? We have customers!"

Joey waved his arm at the prep station, his face a picture of innocence. "I'm right where I'm supposed to be. She's the one throwing things."

With Mr. Barnes standing there, I saw my chance. I knew I couldn't keep up with Joey's verbal attacks. And I knew I couldn't claw that smug smile off his face.

"Joey's right," I said to Mr. Barnes. "I'm the one who should be in the dining room."

Joey smirked. Cam seemed engrossed in the stainless-steel surface of the prep table.

"But I think Joey would rather be out there bussing tables," I said. "There's more money in it. Isn't that right, Joey?"

Joey's sneer froze on his face. That was all the encouragement I needed to keep going.

"Did you ever notice how eager he is to help out in the dining room?" I asked Mr. Barnes. "He moves pretty fast when it comes to snatching things off tables."

And now his cocky grin started melting away.

Mr. Barnes's eyes flitted from me to Joey and back to me. "What are you talking about, Tera? Did you see something?"

"I saw him take something from a table," I said.

Joey rubbed the back of his neck. "She's full of shit."

I shrugged, like he might have a point. "And did you know he drinks beer all night from the tap?"

Mr. Barnes looked furious. "We'll talk about this later. Right now we're in the middle of dinner rush, and I need all of you to get back to work."

Before I headed to the dining room, I tried to catch Cam's eye. I needed to know if I'd just ruined whatever friendship we had.

Cam didn't see me. He was kneeling on the floor picking up my pen. He stood and held it out. "You dropped this."

My hand shook as I took it from him. "Thanks."

"Do you need anything?" he asked, always with that shy politeness.

Tears of relief welled up behind my eyes. Relief because he was still being nice to me after all he'd heard. "I'm good," I said.

And then I went back to work.

● ● ●

After the dinner rush, Mr. Barnes called Joey back to his office. Cam, Sadie, and I huddled near the prep table, hoping to listen in, but Mr. Barnes had made sure to shut his door.

Sadie peered at my face. "I know you hate him. And you have every right to. But tell me for real. You saw him stealing tips from the tables?"

"I saw him take something from *your* table," I said. It didn't seem to matter that I wasn't sure what he'd taken. They assumed it was money. I let them assume.

"Do you think he'll get fired?" Cam asked.

"If Mr. Barnes doesn't fire him," Sadie said, "then I quit. I'm not working with someone who steals from me."

After a few minutes, Joey came out of Mr. Barnes's office. He had a vague smile on his face.

Shit, I thought. *He didn't get fired.*

And then he took off his work apron, wadded it into a ball, and threw it into the garbage. I wanted to cheer.

"Hoo-ray," Cam whispered.

Sadie, Cam, and I lined up against the prep table to watch him leave. Joey didn't look at any of us as he walked past.

I thought of it as his walk of shame.

CHAPTER 31

The sun had barely risen over the tallest downtown buildings when Herman Liebowitz greeted my mom and me in his office the next morning. If he was surprised to see my mom with me, he was polite enough not to say anything.

"Thank you for coming," he said.

He looked exactly how I'd pictured him. An old guy, tall and lean, with thinning white hair and wrinkled skin. I wiped my sweaty palm on my jeans before shaking his hand.

"Won't you sit down?"

Mom and I took seats across from him at a big conference table where a file folder marked *Confidential* lay next to an open laptop. I assumed it was some new evidence against my dad, and suddenly I was glad Mom was there beside me. Whatever was in that folder, I didn't want to deal with it alone.

"Can I get you something to drink?" he asked. "My girl's not in yet, but I think I can manage to get you some coffee."

"No, thanks," Mom said.

I didn't say anything. I couldn't take my eyes off the file folder.

"Then let's get down to business." He folded his hands and placed them in front of him on the table. "I called you in here because I thought you should know about a key piece of evidence we found. It's rather sensitive, and I didn't think it was right to let you hear about it from an outside source."

Suddenly I felt sure I knew what was in that folder. "The picture," I murmured.

He leaned closer. "I'm sorry, what was that?"

Mom whipped her head toward me. "What are you talking about? What picture?"

I closed my eyes, trying to banish the image of me naked, posing like a dog. I'd tried so hard to forget it, but I knew it too well. Every line, every shadow.

"Miss Waters?"

I opened my eyes to see Herman Liebowitz looking at me. I saw compassion, but I saw confusion, too. He didn't know what I was talking about. So it wasn't the photo of me naked. It was something else. Thank God it was something else.

"I'm okay."

"I know this is difficult for you, but if there's anything you want to tell me . . ."

"Please," I said. "Just show me what's in there."

"All right." He put his hand on the folder but didn't open it.

"This is hard for me to say, and there's no delicate way to put it." He took a deep breath and opened the file folder.

Inside was a graphic novel. On its cover, a drawing of a naked child, a girl of about nine. I recognized my dad's work right away, but it took me a moment longer to realize I was staring at my own face.

The naked girl with my face stood posing in front of a classroom. One thin arm rested on her bare hip. Her other hand held stringy hair off her shoulders. She thrust her chest out, flat as it was, and propped one of her legs on a desk. The pose was designed to give a full view of her nudity, but someone, probably Herman Liebowitz, had stuck a Post-it note over her privates. On the chalkboard behind her, I recognized my dad's careful lettering: *A Bowl Full of Cherries.*

Something inside me withered and turned to dust. My throat swelled up. Tears stung my eyes but didn't fall. Under the table, Mom grabbed my hand and held on.

A moment of silence, and then Herman Liebowitz started talking. "Your father wrote and illustrated a series of pornographic books portraying children. There are many different faces in these so-called graphic novels, but the main one is obviously based on Miss Waters, on how she looked as a child of about eight or nine."

He cleared his throat. "There's more inside the book that you don't want to see. Sexual acts." He laid his hand over the cover and looked at each of us in turn. "I'm sorry. I thought you should know."

I stared at the girl's face peeking out from beneath the lawyer's liver-spotted hand. She had a sulking, pouty look, like she'd gotten in trouble. It was a face I knew well. I'd painted it enough times.

"Miss Waters? If there's—"

"Other people saw this?" I asked.

"I'm afraid so."

"He sold it to people?"

"Yes."

A horrible thought came to me. "How much money did he make from it?"

"He sold a series of these . . . books. Not all of them featured children. Some of them were adult pornography. I guess you could say he specialized in portraying fetishes. People pay a lot to see their sexual fantasies in print."

"How much?" I repeated. "How much did he make?"

"The investigation is still ongoing, but we estimate he made anywhere from twenty to thirty thousand dollars over the years. He had quite a little enterprise going."

Twenty thousand dollars. About the same amount he had given me for art school. Under the table, my mom's hand squeezed harder.

"Miss Waters, I know this is difficult for you. The way the law is . . . This is simulated pornography, and it came out before 2003."

My mom's voice was shaky. "What's that got to do with it?"

"That's when a federal law was passed, making it illegal to simulate child pornography."

"So you're saying this isn't illegal because he did it before 2003?"

"It's a gray area. But with Miss Waters's face as one of the victims . . . It becomes less gray."

Mom grabbed the file folder and slammed it closed. "How can this *not* be illegal? How?"

"I didn't say it wasn't illegal. I said it was debatable. But his timing was perfect, as if he knew exactly what the law would allow and deliberately worked around it. It was after 2003 that he stopped drawing children and began producing books depicting other types of fetishes."

I listened to all of this like I was detached from my own body. The words hung there, waiting to be heard, while my thoughts reeled, trying to process what I'd seen. My dad had drawn me naked. That much was on the cover. And inside those pages . . . What was I doing? Posing so men could get off? Having sex with them? Did he show me liking it, or was I crying and pleading with them to stop?

All my life I'd clung to him, practically begged him to love me. But now I knew I'd never been a daughter to him. I was something else. Whatever he wanted me to be, that's what I was for him. A lump of clay to be shaped. Something to be sold to strangers so they could—

"Tera?" Mom cut into my thoughts. "Tera, look at me."

I blinked, my eyes like sandpaper.

"Can I get you a glass of water?" asked Mr. Liebowitz.

"I'm okay."

"Do you understand what your mother and I were discussing?"

"Yes."

"I want you to know that we can make a federal case, especially since the simulations show a real person. This kind of thing has been an ongoing issue for years, and the laws have been challenged several times."

"You want to show this?" I said. "Make a case out of it?"

"I know how hard this must be for you."

Mom cleared her throat. "He'll still go to prison without anyone seeing it, right? He'll go to prison for the photos that were found on his computer?"

"Most likely."

"Then no one has to see this. We'll make it disappear."

"Mrs. Waters." He was talking to my mom now. "It's debatable whether these books were illegal at the time, but we can still make a stronger case against him. A jury won't like knowing he compromised his daughter this way. I'm gathering other testimony, too." He looked at me. "Your testimony would help immensely."

I wanted to tell him I didn't have any testimony to give, but I'd already let it slip about the picture. He'd want to know the details. If I talked to him, he'd know I'd posed for it willingly. The whole world would know.

He slid his business card across the table to me. "I'm here to see that justice is done."

I stared at the card but didn't take it. "I need to go home."

● ● ●

Mom drove. I didn't think I could.

"You want me to drop you off at school?" she asked.

"I'm not going."

I expected her to argue, but she nodded instead. "What are you going to do?" she asked.

"I don't know."

We didn't talk again until we were almost home. The silence between us felt oddly comforting. I didn't think I could handle empty words.

When she turned onto our street, the mail truck was just arriving at our house.

"I'll grab it," I said, glad for the distraction.

Mom stopped at the top of our driveway and let me out. I couldn't help looking across the street to Haley's house as I pulled the pile of mail from our box. Haley's car was gone. She was at school, of course. I wished I hadn't talked to her yesterday. I wished I hadn't made her cry.

"What's wrong?" Mom asked when I got back in the car.

I shook my head. I didn't want to talk about Haley.

"Did something come in the mail?"

I looked down at the pile of letters in my lap. She saw it before I did. A letter from the prison. From Dad.

"Don't read it," Mom said, but I was already tearing open the envelope. She put the car in park but kept the engine running. "Please don't read it."

I pulled out the single piece of paper.

Dear Tera,

I tried to call you, but you hung up on me, so that's why I'm writing. I called to tell you that you can still go to Paris. Come visit me and I'll explain.

Love,
Dad

"What's he say?" Mom asked.

"He says I can still go to art school, that he can help me."

"He's lying." She studied my face. "You know that, right?"

But I didn't think he was. He probably had more money stashed away from sales of his porn comics.

"He wants me to come visit him," I said.

Her eyes got huge. She looked scared. "You think he wants to *help* you? He wants something from you. He wants to get you in there so he can lie to you."

"I know that," I said. "But I need to go." I needed to tell him I knew about *A Bowl Full of Cherries.*

She lowered her head and pinched the bridge of her nose. "Please, don't," she said.

"I have to, Mom. I'm going."

She twisted in her seat to face me. "Let me go with you then. I can help you."

I shook my head. I didn't want her there when I confronted him.

"I helped you today, didn't I?" She stared out the front window at the sloping driveway. "You needed me there."

"Yeah, Mom." I wanted to touch her hand. Instead, I stuffed Dad's letter back into the envelope. "I'm glad you went with me today."

"So you'll let me go with you to see him?"

"No." I shook my head. "I need to do this by myself."

Her lips tightened. Her hand squeezed the gearshift. "When will you go?"

"Tonight." Dad's cellblock allowed visitors on Tuesday evenings.

"I wish you'd let me go with you."

When I didn't say anything, she shifted into drive, and we rolled the rest of the way down the driveway. She turned off the car and grabbed my hand, squeezing it hard before letting me go.

CHAPTER 32

The Best Gift Ever

Her dad handed her a box wrapped in Christmas paper, only it wasn't Christmas. It was her seventeenth birthday. The box was small and rectangle-shaped. A necklace, maybe? But her dad wasn't the type to buy her jewelry. Another paintbrush, then. A really good one.

"Can I open it now?" She glanced at her mom. Her mom was the one who would flip out if she opened the gift when she wasn't supposed to.

Her mom nodded, even smiled a little. "Hurry up before the pizza gets cold."

"Any guesses?" asked her dad.

She gave the box a little shake. Heavy and solid, not like a paintbrush at all. "New acrylics?"

"Wrong! Guess again."

Her mom sighed.

"I don't know . . . A chocolate bar?"

"That's your guess? Really?"

"Just let her open it, Tim."

"Fine." He waved his hand at her. "Go ahead."

She made a tear in the shiny wrapping, peeled it away, and let it fall to the floor. Her mom snatched it up and wadded it into a ball.

Tera held a small box with the name of a bank on it. "You robbed a bank?" she joked.

"Open it."

She did. At first she thought it was money inside, a nice fat stack. But then she saw it was the wrong color, the wrong everything. "What is it?" she asked.

Her dad lifted the stack of bills from the box and riffled them. "This is your future," he said. "Savings bonds. They'll mature next year."

Her mouth dropped open. "For art school?"

"The one in France, if you can get in. It took me a long time to save that much."

"Oh my God, thank you!" She threw her arms around his neck and hugged him as hard as she could. He patted her on the back, whispered in her ear. "I love you."

His arms felt strong and good, and she closed her eyes, wanting to melt into the feeling. When she opened them, she saw how her mom was staring at her and biting her lip. She moved to give her mom a hug, too, but her mom shook her head, crossed her arms over her chest.

"Don't thank me," she said. "I had nothing to do with it."

CHAPTER 33

The concrete walls of the visiting room seemed to close in on me as I sat down in one of the hard chairs that lined the wall of bullet-proof glass. I couldn't stop shaking. Maybe this wasn't such a good idea.

A door opened on the other side. I blew on my cold hands and squinted through the hazy glass at the man in the orange jumpsuit trudging toward me. He moved slowly, his body stiff as he sat across from me and picked up his phone.

I stared. This was my dad, but his face was so battered that I barely recognized him. He had a gash above one eye, with angry black stitches cutting through red, swollen skin. The flesh around his cheekbones looked mushy, like chewed-up meat, and one side of his mouth was bloated like an inner tube.

I lifted the receiver and brought it to my ear. "Dad, what happened to you?" As much as I despised him, he was still my dad.

"They beat the shit out of me, that's what happened." His words came out slurred and mangled.

"Who did?" I asked, even though I was pretty sure I knew the answer. "When?"

"Yesterday."

So, this had happened after he wrote me the letter.

"A bunch of prisoners jumped me in the exercise yard." He touched his swollen lips like it hurt for him to talk. "Guys on their third strike, with no chance of getting out. They said they'd kill me."

"No one's going to kill you." I tried to sound reassuring, but I knew all about the prison hierarchy, how child molesters were the lowest of the low. "Tell the guards what happened," I said. "They'll protect you."

He barked a laugh. "The guards are the ones who put them up to it. They told me I was headed to prison for sure. Said they wanted to give me a preview of what it would be like."

"They can't do that."

He leaned back in his chair and laughed. "Open your fucking eyes, Tera."

Good advice. If only I'd opened them sooner.

"So what do you want from me?" I asked. "Your letter said you could help me go to art school. But I know that's not why you called me here."

"That's exactly why I called you here. But then this happened." He pointed to his mangled face. "I'm not going to lie to you. I'm scared. I was ready, before, to take my chances with the public defender. But now . . . I need that lawyer."

"You told me you didn't think she could help you."

"At the time, I didn't think she could. When Chase Hardy told me what they found on my computer, he said there was no way I could fight it. But then this new lawyer comes along and says I can. I never told you I was guilty, Tera. You assumed that. And I'm telling you now . . . Those downloads were an accident."

I studied him through the glass. Did he honestly think I believed him?

"You have to help me, Tera. You have to keep paying Charlotte Gross so I can get out of here. If I don't have a good lawyer, I'm going to prison for sure. And I won't last in there. You know I won't last."

Something didn't make sense. "You said in your letter you could send me to art school," I said. "How were you planning to do that?"

He stared at me like he didn't understand the question.

"I'm thinking you must have some money stashed away," I said. "And if that's the case, you can pay for your own lawyer."

He leaned forward in his chair so his face was inches from the glass. "Before I get into that, I want to tell you something."

I gripped the phone a little tighter. This sounded like a confession. "Tell me," I said.

"They record everything we say. I need you to understand what that means."

It meant he didn't want to say anything that might incriminate him. "Then what am I doing here?" I asked. "I came here to see what you had to say. And to tell you I know about the—"

He cut me off. "You're right. I have money."

"So what's the problem? If you have money, you don't need my help."

"I *had* money. They froze my account while they investigate where the money came from."

"Because you earned it illegally."

"No! I'll admit, I made money penning some pretty racy comics."

"Racy comics?" Why wouldn't he just say it?

"Okay, pornographic comics. But nothing illegal, I swear."

And in that, he might be telling the truth. Herman Liebowitz had said the comics with children in them weren't considered illegal because of how the law was back then.

"So when this is all over," he said, "they'll unfreeze my account. And you can have the money. You can still go to Paris."

I leaned forward, staring at him through the glass. "I don't want your money."

"Why not? It's—"

"Because I know how you earned it."

He made a dismissive gesture with his hand.

"I know you drew me, Dad. I know you sold me."

His body got very still.

"Yeah, Dad. I know about *A Bowl Full of Cherries*."

His eyes dropped to his hands. He rubbed his fingers together. Slowly, he shook his head. "I don't know what you think I did, but you can't talk about that here. Wait until we're sitting down with Charlotte Gross and then we can talk about it. The truth, okay? But we'll only get the truth if I have a good lawyer. Charlotte Gross is good. You were smart to hire her."

"So you're saying everything I think about you is a mistake?"

"There's two sides to everything, Tera. If I get sent to State, I'm a dead man. You know that."

"So you want me to keep paying the lawyer."

"And I want you to sit down with her, with both of us. So I can explain what really happened."

"Tell me now what happened."

"I can't. They're listening."

I glared at him through the glass. This was pointless. He was never going to admit to anything.

"Dammit, Tera. You're smarter than this. Think! Think about what you know about me. All your life I did what I thought was best for you. Since you could hold a crayon in your hand, I saw what you could be. I worked my whole life to make you into a great artist. And I protected you."

I kept shaking my head.

"I did, Tera. You don't realize how crazy your mom is. You don't know how she tried to rub her craziness off on you. Even now, she can get to you."

"No one's getting to me."

"It's true. She's like a disease that creeps under your skin."

The fingers of his free hand crawled up his arm, as if to show me how insidious Mom could be. My throat closed up as I watched him. His fingers were stained with ink. They'd always been that way, ever since I could remember. I used to love watching those hands move over blank paper, creating something from nothing.

And that's how he had created me. On clean paper, he made an image of me that he could stare at whenever he wanted. He could have drawn me playing. He could have drawn me laughing. Instead, he drew me naked.

That picture of me on the cover of his porn comic, stripped to nothing, with my leg propped on a desk. Like he was inviting all his friends to have me. *A Bowl Full of Cherries*, ripe for the eating. I'd been trying not to think about what was inside those pages. Naked little girls. Naked men. Men with little girls.

He'd stopped talking.

"I'm leaving," I said. I stood.

"You can't!" On the other side of the glass, he reached for me.

I knew he couldn't touch me, but I cringed from his hand.

"Please," he said.

Feedback on the phone echoed my voice. "Is that what I said in your graphic novels?"

He furrowed his brow, gave a warning shake of his head.

"Did I say, *'Please'*?"

"You don't know what you're talking about."

"When the men had me backed into a corner in your fantasy world, did I say, *'Please don't'*? Or maybe you had me saying something else. *'Please fuck me'*?"

"You're wrong. Stop talking."

"Did you draw yourself as a character, too?"

"Tera, shut up!"

"Did you put your hand over my mouth to stop me from talking? Did you actually draw yourself pounding into me?"

"Guard!" he called. "We're done!"

The guard was on his way, but Dad kept the phone pressed to his ear.

"Do you tell yourself you sold me to help me out? Is that how you justify it? Or maybe you think you never hurt me. All you did was *draw* me—and then maybe take the drawing into the bathroom with you so you could jerk off? What could be the harm in that?"

"I said, shut up!"

A guard took the phone out of my hand. Another guard on the other side took my dad's arm, started to lead him away. He was still talking to me, even though I couldn't hear him. But I saw his lips moving. *Tera! Don't do this! I never wanted to hurt you!*

And then he was gone from my sight.

"This way," the guard said.

I followed the guard through the twisty corridors. A steel door slammed shut behind me. The clang echoed against the stone walls. Sealing my dad away.

CHAPTER 34

As soon as I got home from the prison, I poured myself a huge glass of water from the jug in the fridge. I couldn't remember ever feeling so thirsty, and I stood there with the refrigerator door hanging open and gulped it down.

I was pouring myself a second glass when Mom came into the kitchen. She'd curled her hair. It made her look younger. "How'd it go?" she asked.

I shut the refrigerator. "I did it. I stood up to him." I opened the drawer and pulled out the scrap of paper where I'd written Herman Liebowitz's number. I held it up for Mom to see. "I'm going to call him. I'm going to testify."

Her face sagged. "You don't have to do that. There's no reason anyone has to know about that filth."

"He's going to show them in court. He'll subpoena me if I don't talk to him."

"I don't understand what he wants from you." She rubbed her hand over her eyes, like she was trying to erase her memory. "What can you tell him that he doesn't already know?"

There was something I could tell him, but I wasn't ready to say it out loud. I sat down at the kitchen table to think. Mom sat beside me. I felt her eyes on me.

I could tell him about the photo, how I'd undressed for my dad and gotten on my hands and knees. I'd been probing that memory for years. I'd touch it, and then I'd flinch away.

If I told him about the photo, there'd be no more pretending it hadn't affected me. No more pretending Dad had done it because he didn't know any better.

And what would happen if I didn't tell? What if my dad's new lawyer picked up where Charlotte Gross had left off? What if my dad got set free because his lawyer argued that he "accidentally" downloaded child pornography? Would the porn comics be enough to convict him? Maybe not. Herman Liebowitz had said it was debatable whether they were even illegal.

I imagined my dad coming home after his trial. For him, it would all be over, like waking from a bad dream. And how would he explain himself to me? Would he find some other way to manipulate me? What if he started preying on little kids? Maybe he'd been doing that all along.

"Mom," I said. "There's something I have to tell you."

She stopped rubbing her eyes and lifted her head.

"You know how Dad always wanted me to draw nudes?"

She froze, waiting for me to say it.

"I posed for him, Mom."

I knew I would never forget her face. She was like that woman in the Bible who looked back at her village being destroyed. She was a pillar of salt, with glassy, staring eyes and an open mouth.

I tried to make it sound reasonable, the way he'd made it sound to me. "He wanted me to practice drawing nudes. He told me I could practice on myself, like a self-portrait. So I let him take a photo of me . . . and then I sketched myself."

"Oh, Tera."

"I only let him do it one time." I covered my face with my hands so she wouldn't have to look at me. "I knew it was wrong, and the next time he tried it, I kicked and cried. So it was only that one time that he took a photo. I swear."

I heard her rapid breathing, but she didn't say anything. She didn't touch me.

"I hate myself for letting him do that."

A pause, and then she whispered: "Don't."

I cried into my hands, still not able to look at her. After a minute, I felt her touch on my shoulder, hesitant.

"It's not your fault," she said. "It's mine."

I'd been longing to hear her say that. I didn't know how badly until then. She said it again—*It's not your fault*—and I pressed my head against her chest and sobbed.

• • •

Mom wanted to talk more, but when I glanced out the window and saw Haley's Audi pull into her driveway, I told Mom I'd be back in a few minutes. There was something I had to do.

I hadn't seen Haley since I'd made her cry. Now I knew why she was so upset. Because Herman Liebowitz had shown her what was inside those porn comics—only he hadn't shown her pictures of me.

A Bowl Full of Cherries—as in, more than one. Dad had put Haley on those pages, too.

I walked across the street and rang Haley's doorbell. Westminster chimes. I hadn't heard that sing-song tune in a long time, not since I used to play at her house when we were kids. I always felt jealous because her doorbell sounded so peaceful.

Her mom opened the door and almost shut it in my face when she saw me, but I heard Haley's voice call out. "It's okay, Mom. I'll talk to her."

Mrs. Sweeney hesitated before moving aside. I was sure I could read her thoughts: *Who's this piece of trash setting foot in my lovely house?*

Haley led me to her room and closed the door. She had the same pink canopy over her bed that she'd had when we were kids. Posters of heavy-metal bands covered her walls instead of the boy bands she'd liked when we were friends.

She sat down on her bed and hugged her knees. I stood in the middle of the room.

"I came to apologize," I said. "For the other day."

Her eyes got wide. "You were a total bitch to me."

"I know."

"I hate your dad. I hate the way you think he's so awesome." She straightened her legs and lifted her chin. "You still think it, don't you? You have no idea what a fucked-up creep he is."

"I do," I said. "I know."

She snorted.

"The lawyer told me about the porn comics," I said.

Our eyes met for just an instant before we both looked away.

"It's fucked up," she said.

"Yeah."

Her fingers dug into her bedspread. "I want him to die. If I could get to him, I'd kill him. But you want to help him."

"I don't want to help him. Not anymore. I know what he did now. I didn't know before."

She studied me. "He drew you, too?"

I didn't say anything. She could tell by my face.

"Some fun, huh?"

"Yeah."

She grabbed her pillow and hugged it. "I thought you knew how he came on to me when we were kids. I thought you always knew."

"No."

"Then I'm sorry for thinking that," she said.

"What did he do?" I didn't want to know, but I had to know.

She stared at one of her posters and picked at a loose thread on her bedspread. "He tried one time to get me to sit on his lap. And he'd ask questions about my body. If I had hair down there yet—sick stuff like that. I wasn't even sure what he was doing, but I knew it wasn't right. I was a kid. You know?"

I nodded. I knew.

There was a long silence before she spoke. "I'm sorry I was such a bitch all the time."

"I get it."

"When we were little, I used to tell you I thought your dad was creepy, but you'd tell me to shut up."

I didn't remember that.

"It was so stupid, the way you protected him. I thought you liked it."

"Liked it?"

"I thought you let him do stuff to you."

"Why would you think that?"

"You didn't?"

"No!" The denial came automatically.

"Oh," she said.

I wrapped my arms around my chest and looked at the floor. If I couldn't tell her the truth, I'd never be able to testify in front of a court. And I *wanted* her to know, because I was sick of hiding in the shadow of this thing that had happened when I was nine years old.

So I lifted my head, and I blurted it out. "I lied. He took a picture of me. I let him."

She stared at me. "That's horrible."

"I was so stupid."

She moved to the edge of the bed, reached out her hand, but all I wanted was to fold myself in half like a sheet of paper. Fold myself into smaller and smaller pieces.

She grabbed my hand and pulled me down beside her. We sat on the edge of her bed and stared at the pink rug at our feet. "I didn't mean *you* were horrible," she said. "I meant . . ." She squeezed my hand. "It's horrible that he did that to you. You were just a kid. You didn't 'let' him do anything."

"I could have stopped him. He tried again another time and I wouldn't let him."

"How'd you stop him?"

"I cried."

And then I started laughing.

She laughed, too. "God, that's fucked up."

It was.

She let go of my hand so she could press her palms into her thighs. "After your dad got all creepy, I didn't want to hang out with you. But I didn't have to treat you that way."

I shrugged.

"And it wasn't me who posted on the forum. RubyQueen15. That's Ellen Cornwell."

"Oh." That made sense.

Haley brushed her hands down her cheeks. "I haven't stopped crying since I saw those pictures he drew."

"I'm sorry."

"It's not your fault."

Those words again. I looked behind me at her closed door. "I should go."

"Yeah." She stood up. "Are we okay, Tera? I don't hate you or anything."

"I don't hate you either."

She laughed again, and so did I. It felt good to laugh.

• • •

As soon as I got home, I went downstairs to my dad's studio. Everything I needed was down there: canvas, brushes, paint . . . and my dad's shadow. I sat in front of a blank canvas.

I saw myself as a nine-year-old girl, waiting in her room for her father to come to her. He wanted to see the drawing she'd done, the one of her with no clothes on, when she'd pretended to be a dog. She wanted to tear it up, but he had to judge it first. She hoped it was good enough. She wanted him to be proud of her.

He came to her and looked at her drawing and said it wasn't good enough, the girl on her hands and knees, naked like a skinned animal. He wanted her to do it again, to strip and pose. He wanted her to be proud of what she was doing.

But the shame still pulsed from her eyes, her fingers, her mouth. The shame that made her want to hide herself away.

He got mad when she told him no. He didn't like how she struggled when he took her shirt off. He said she was crazy like her mom. Said he was sick of her.

"I'm so sick of you."

So she tried. She tried very, very hard to do what he wanted. So he wouldn't be sick of her. So he'd be proud of her and love her.

The memory came out through my brushstrokes. The colors I put on the canvas came from inside me. Purple like a bruise, red like dried blood, muddy gray and black, colors slick and crusty and textured like a scab.

The girl lay on the bed. The man hovered over her, his face clouded by a smoky halo, arms slick up to the elbow, pulling out what was small and good, pulling it out like a butcher pulls guts from a slaughtered pig.

The girl on her back, kicking like a bug, her head thrown back, her mouth stretched open—too far. Her jaw unhinged.

● ● ●

A long time later, I laid my paintbrush down and closed my eyes. When I opened them, the memory I'd been living with—the one I wanted to disappear—lay right there in front of me. But it wasn't inside me anymore. It was out of me for good.

I breathed through my nose, enjoying the tacky smell of paint. My brushes lay scattered on my tray, each one unique, each with its own memory attached. Gifts from my dad.

I looked back at my painting of the man and the girl—me and my dad—each of us trying to get what we wanted.

Want, I thought, and carefully printed the title on the bottom right corner. Under that, I signed my name.

CHAPTER 35

"Tera!" Mom's voice drifted through the open window of Dad's studio. "Don't you have to get ready for work?" The house was sold, but she'd been outside all morning, clipping away with her pruning shears. Gardening was part of her therapy.

"Cam's not coming until four-thirty!" I called.

I left the half-finished painting on its easel and looked around at my scattered drawings, at the open tubes of paint and dirty paintbrushes. Dad liked things in their proper places. Every brush had to be cleaned and put away, every sketch kept neat and flat and sealed in a drawer. If he could see his studio now, he'd be disappointed in me. He'd shake his head in disgust.

A breeze blew through the open window. Lilacs and roses. Much better than stale cigarette smoke. I wondered if my dad could smell flowers from his cell in solitary, where they'd put him for his own protection. Not that he was ever into green stuff. He used to make fun of my mom for spending so much time in her garden. Maybe in ten to fifteen years, after breathing nothing but concrete and bleach . . . maybe then he'd appreciate the crisp scent of freshly mown grass.

"Tera?" My mom's voice again, right outside the window. She sounded nervous. "Someone's here."

I glanced at my watch. Way too early for Cam. So who could it be? Another reporter asking about Dad?

A car door slammed. Footsteps on gravel. A man's voice, talking to Mom.

I couldn't hear what they were saying, but Mom sounded guarded. She didn't need this right now. She didn't need some reporter coming over to talk about my dad. His trial was done. He was gone. That was it.

The screen door groaned open and shut. The ceiling creaked as footsteps crossed over the kitchen floor. Whoever it was, she'd invited him inside. Then the door at the top of the stairs squeaked open.

Mom's voice called down. "Tera?"

I moved to the foot of the stairs. Mom's anxious face peered down at me. "There's someone here to see you."

A man stepped up behind her. Not Cam. And not a reporter. It was Mr. Stewart. He smiled at me and waved. "It's good to see you, Tera. Mind if I come down for a minute?" He started down the stairs with Mom right behind him.

I rubbed my hands on my jeans, pushed my hair back. What would he think of me? I hadn't seen him in months, not since graduation.

He stepped off the bottom stair. His eyes bounced over the room. "This is where you work?" he asked.

I shrugged, self-conscious of the mess. "Not for long," I said. "We're moving."

Mr. Stewart turned in a slow circle, taking in the dozens of canvases lining the walls. "You've been busy."

"She paints all the time now," Mom said.

"I'm glad to hear that." He kept looking around.

"Not to be rude," Mom said. "But why are you here?"

"I'm sorry." He stopped looking at my paintings and turned to face us. "It's nothing bad. At least I hope it's good."

"What is it?" I asked.

"Well, it's about that contest."

"You said you didn't win," Mom said.

"I didn't. *Girl on a Bus* didn't even place."

"Well, you're right. *Girl on a Bus* didn't win. But when you told me you'd entered something you weren't happy with, I took the liberty of entering one of your other paintings. *Gray Day.* It had rain in it, remember? So it fit the contest's theme."

I remembered. The girl with the scraggly hair, standing with her dog on the playground.

"And I'm glad I entered it," Mr. Stewart said. "Because you won third prize."

Mom opened her mouth. Her eyes teared up.

"I'm sorry it took so long to tell you," he said. "But there was some confusion over whether a third party could enter for someone else. I entered it under your name, but I used my e-mail address. I finally got it straightened out, though. And look." He pulled a check from his pocket and handed it to me. "I know it's not enough to send you to art school or anything, but it'll help, right? I hope you're still planning on going?"

I looked down at the check in my hand. It was made out to me, for a thousand dollars. I swallowed hard so my words wouldn't sound choked. "I'm saving up," I said.

"That's great."

It wasn't great. By now, I should have been packing my bags to study art in Paris. But it was a start. The world wasn't perfect.

"Thanks for doing this," I said. "Thanks for doing what I should have done."

"You're welcome." He smiled. I smiled back.

Mom broke the silence. "So someone show me how she won a thousand dollars. What did you enter?"

"Oh, right." Mr. Stewart pulled out his phone and started swiping through photos. "It's called *Gray Day.* She dropped it off in my classroom one day, before we even knew about the contest."

I remembered. The same day I'd asked him to bail out my dad from jail.

"Here is it." He handed the phone to my mom and tapped on the screen to enlarge the image. For the first time, I noticed how scared the girl looked. She was depending on her dog to protect her, but maybe the dog wasn't doing such a good job.

"This is the painting I wanted to see in that article about you and your dad," Mr. Stewart said. "I know you were disappointed the article never saw print."

I shrugged. It seemed like such a long time ago.

"But I have another bit of good news. *ArtWorld* is going to run a feature on the contest winners. First, second, and third place. They all get write-ups in the magazine, plus pictures of their work."

Mom's smile was huge. I smiled, too. "Your friend's still the editor?" I said.

"Well, yes. But she wanted to do this. It'll be a great story. And it'll look really good when you apply to art school. Not that you'd have any trouble getting in. Did you check scholarships for next year?"

"Not yet." I shook my head, embarrassed. "I guess I need someone to motivate me."

"It looks like you're motivated to paint, at least." His eyes wandered the room, taking in the stacks of paintings I'd done in the past months. I'd been on a creative streak, but a lot of them were only half-finished. Some of them I'd given up on altogether. Now I wished I had something solid to show him.

"Tera! My God!"

"What?" Mom sounded panicked. "What's wrong?"

His mouth was open like he was in shock. I followed his gaze to one of my paintings. *Want.*

Slowly, he walked toward it. Mom and I trailed behind.

It wasn't a large painting—about the size of a poster board—but it stood out. As I watched him study it, I saw my work with fresh eyes. The shadowy man hovering over the girl, pulling out tendrils from her kicking body. The girl's mouth stretched wide in a silent cry. All the colors muted and grayed, what I imagined to be colors of pain.

Mr. Stewart leaned in, examining the details. "It reminds me of William Blake's work." I saw what he was getting at. All those paintings with anguished faces, bodies crouched and suffering. All those poems about innocence lost.

"You like it?" Mom asked him.

"Absolutely."

Mom squinted at it. To her, it would look ugly, but I knew what Mr. Stewart was seeing. He saw all those parts of me that had gone into creating it. Shame, pity, love. Most of all, love—not for my grown-up self—but for the little girl in the painting.

"It's you, isn't it?" Mr. Stewart asked me. "The girl in the painting?"

I nodded. They were all me, in some shape or form. They were all self-portraits.

"It's beautiful," he said, and I couldn't help smiling a little, because I knew he was talking about me.